BUFFALO BRIGADE

ROCKY MOUNTAIN SAINT BOOK 10

B.N. RUNDELL

WOLFPACK
PUBLISHING
— EST 2013 —

Buffalo Brigade
(Rocky Mountain Saint Book 10)
B.N. Rundell

Paperback Edition
© Copyright 2019 B.N. Rundell

Wolfpack Publishing
6032 Wheat Penny Avenue
Las Vegas, NV 89122

Paperback ISBN 978-1-64119-506-5
eBook ISBN 978-1-64119-505-8

Library of Congress Control Number: 2019932475

To those who have gone before . . .
To blaze the trails, to carve the way, and to lay the foundations.
To those wo will come after . . .
May you make something better out of what you've been left.
To those who will read these words . . .
May you have a moment's respite, a touch of a smile, a bit of an escape.
Thank you and God bless you, one and all.

BUFFALO BRIGADE

CHAPTER ONE
LEAVING

THE LATE SPRING STORM WAS SHOWING NO MERCY. THE howling winds drove the heavy wet flakes against Tate and his grulla gelding, Shady. Both had their heads tucked down, Tate had the collar of his buffalo hide coat turned up to meet the downturned brim of his hat. The wool scarf, knit from the undercoat of the buffalo, held his hat secure and his mittens were stiff with the blast. The end of his scarf wrapped around his chin, covering his nose, but was layered with the wet, icy snow. Breathing was difficult, seeing nigh unto impossible. The flatlands of Nebraska Territory offered little shelter from the last gasp of a hard winter.

Tate and his family left their cabin in the Wind River Mountains at the first sign of spring. A storm like this would be commonplace in the mountains, but the flowers had already burst through the crust of dry soil and were showing their color here in the plains. Lobo, the big grey wolf and Tate's long-time companion, had his head tilted away from the blizzard's blast as he walked alongside the grulla. Tate's family, his redheaded Irish wife, Maggie and their two youngsters, Sadie, the girl at age eight who thought she was twenty, and Sean, the big strapping boy of thirteen who constantly followed in his father's footsteps, were with the freighters and wagons that followed Tate's lead. They were traveling east on the Oregon Trail, carrying a load of pelts and Indian trade goods from Fort Bernard and Fort Laramie, bound for St. Louis.

Suddenly, Shady bumped against a mound of white that grunted and moved away slowly. Tate reined up, looking around, shading his eyes from the snow and squinted. Buffalo! The grunts and occasional bellow from a cow searching for her newborn confirmed his dim eyesight. He reached down and patted the side of Shady's neck, talking into his ear, "Easy boy, them buffler's a sight bigger'n us." They could be in the middle of a small bunch of twenty or edging into a massive herd of two thousand; there was no way of knowing. But small or large, a herd of buffalo could easily make mincemeat of him and his animals if they were spooked. He spoke just loud enough for Lobo to hear, "C'mon boy, let's back out o' these woolies." He pulled Shady's head up and leaned back in the saddle, feet extended, which the grulla understood as he started backstepping.

Within moments, they were away from the buffalo and Tate reined Shady to the left toward the cottonwoods at the edge of the Platte River. Although he couldn't see the woods, he knew they were close and would provide the needed protection. The big trees loomed before him as if they sprung from the storm as towering specters of the white-out. He let Shady have his head to pick his own way into the sheltering woods. It was a thick band of the rough-barked trees, and they stood as a barrier to the storm. Tate stepped off his mount, ground tied the gelding and started gathering the downed limbs and branches to get a fire started. Usually careful with the size of a campfire, he abandoned that idea in favor of a signa fire for the wagons.

With his hastily gathered firewood, he soon had a pyramid of kindling beside his tinder, and he knelt before the pile, spread his buffalo coat wide as a windbreak, and struck the steel across the edge of his flint, sparks hit the tinder and glowed. He dropped down to gently blow the glowing ember to flame, added the small kindling, and soon had a warm blaze going. He fed the fire until it was a sizeable inferno that would attract the attention of the coming wagons.

With the blaze going, he tended to Shady, stripped the gear and rubbed him down with a handful of dried grass. The horse had found shelter behind a cluster of cottonwoods and was glad for the relief from the storm. Tate snatched up his saddlebags and returned to the fire with a coffee pot in hand, thoughts of a steaming cup of java making him salivate.

It was about a half hour later when the rattle of trace chains penetrated the howling of the storm, and Tate knew the wagons were coming near. The lead wagon was driven by trader John Richards with the American Fur Company, the man in charge of this train. His covered wagon also had Maggie and Sadie aboard, with Sean riding his Appaloosa alongside. Pulled by four mules, the leader's wagon was one of four in the train. The other twelve were freight wagons, each pulled by a six-up of mules and handled by a teamster with one helper on top. The sixteen wagons lined out in a double row making an arch out from the tree line. With the trees and the river on one side and the wagons on the other, the campsite would soon blossom into a flurry of activity as other cookfires flared.

Tate helped Maggie and Sadie down as Richards stepped to the ground on the opposite side. He turned to Tate, "Ain't it a little early to be stoppin', even with the storm, we could make a few more miles!"

"Prob'ly could, but there's a big herd of buffler that might argue that point!"

"Oh, well, then maybe after this norther blows itself out, we could get some fresh meat!"

"That's what I was thinkin'. Been a while since I had me some buffler tongue!"

Tate Saint and his family had been on the move for a little over a month and were facing more than another before they would reach St. Louis. The plan was for Sadie to start her formal education that she had been begging for since she learned to read at her mother's knee at but four years old. With her hunger for learning and her mother's concern for her safety living in the mountains in the middle of Indian country, the decision had been made, somewhat begrudgingly, to give the city life and education a try. Sean had no interest in the inside of a school room, gaining his education at his father's side in the wilderness. And he was an exceptional student and to look at him; most would think him a full-grown man. He was the mirror image of his father, standing a touch over five and a half feet tall and with shoulders that seemed to widen with every meal that failed to satiate his appetite. His wide grin flashed white teeth and dimples on both cheeks under green eyes that sparkled with mischief. His dark hair hung to his shoulders, and his buckskin-clad frame over a wide stance showed confidence and character.

The decision as to whether Tate and Sean would stay in the city or return to the mountains would not be made until the future for Maggie and Sadie had been settled. Maggie wanted the family to stay together, but she also knew that her man and son would probably never fit into civilization and the crowds of the city. But she was hopeful, nevertheless. It was the love for her daughter that made this trip necessary, but her love for her son and her husband was just as strong.

Sometimes, sacrifices had to be made. Tate had often told her, "Love is self-sacrifice. In the Bible in John 3:16, '*For God so loved the world that He gave . . . '* that's where God Himself defines love. It is self-sacrifice, and that sacrifice when motivated by love, has no limits." As she thought about it, her shoulders heaved, and she drew a deep breath, remembering the words he spoke over their table in the cabin, holding her hand.

She looked into the flames of the fire as she puttered about, preparing their meal of broiled venison, beans, cornbread, and coffee. She enjoyed these times together in the wild, but the world was changing faster than she wanted to admit. With so many of the natives rising up against the encroaching settlers, it wasn't safe in the mountains any longer. They had many fond memories and friends among the different tribes, and she had learned the language of several different people.The leaders of the natives saw their way of life being changed and their lands taken from them, and they believed they must fight for their homes and their families. Their thinking wasn't any different than Maggie's, who felt it necessary to do whatever was required for the safety and security of her family. She glanced up to see Tate watching her, somber as he sat on the log, warming his hands at the fire, but she knew he was thinking about what their future would hold. Their eyes held, understanding, hoping, and wondering.

THE BIG BOOM OF THE SHARPS STARTLED THE CAMP, AND several rolled out of their blankets, grabbing for weapons as they scanned their surroundings for the source of the alarm. Maggie, snug in her blankets, had recognized the loud report and knew Tate had probably scored a hit on a buffalo. When he nudged her awake earlier, he said he was going after some fresh meat, and she knew buffalo was his favorite. She tucked her hands behind her head as she looked up at the bottom of the wagon from her bedroll. She knew she should roll out and get the fire going and the coffee on, but she snuggled down for a few moments in the cool of the morning. But when the Sharps barked again, she sat up, almost hitting her head on the running gear, but she scooted out and stood, looking in the direction of the reports. Again, the Sharps sounded, and a few seconds more, the big buffalo rifle roared twice again.

Several of the freighters and others were standing with rifles at the ready, some nervously walking out from the wagons squinting to see into the grey light of early morning.

John Richards stepped to Maggie's side, "That is Tate shootin', ain't it?"

"Yes. At least that's a Sharps, and that's what he's shooting. But he usually takes down a buffalo with one shot. Something's wrong for him to be shooting so much. We can't use more'n one buffalo," answered Maggie, her brow furrowing as she tried to see through the dim light and the slow rolling fog. It was common on an unusually cold morning for the mist from the river to turn into a thin fog, at least until the morning sun would burn it off, but now it hampered them. The men that had walked out from the wagons returned to the cover of the freighters, and Richards asked, "Didja see anything?"

"Nope, didn't hear nothin' either, leastways not after them last shots. Ain't that Tate out there?" answered the teamster known as Bucky. He was a big man, scruffy, buck teeth, and thick whiskers, well-known as the friendly sort, but not as a man you wanted to cross.

"Yeah, but he hadn't oughta be shootin' so much. Might be trouble. You fellers take up some cover and give it a while. We'll wait'n see what happens. Foolish to go out in this, we'd be shootin' at anything an' ever'thing." He turned to Maggie, "I'm sure he's alright. He can take care o' himself."

Maggie nodded her head, knowing her man was more than capable. But she also knew that anyone could be surprised and overwhelmed in a fog like this, but she wasn't worried, at least not yet.

Sean moved beside his ma, "That's Pa, right Ma?"

Maggie looked at her son, the boy she had nurtured now stood as tall as her and showed himself as much a man as most. She nodded to answer his question but instinctively knew what he would do, and she watched as he trotted back to where their horses were picketed and grabbed his saddle and started rigging his long-legged Appaloosa stallion.The images of the boy and his horse, always inseparable as they had grown together and intuitively anticipated one another's actions, came in a pleasant remembrance and with a touch of envy. Without touching the stirrup, Sean swung aboard and slipped his Hawken into the scabbard as the horse dug dirt to leap away from the wagons.

THERE WAS no mistaking where the buffalo had grazed through the night. The snow had been pushed aside with their noses or scratched away with their hooves. The buffalo is a resilient creature and could find graze where other animals would wander around looking for something without working for it, and the big bison would dig and grub for their life's sustenance. Even in the dim light and wispy fog, their passing was evident. The herd had not moved far, and the shaggy coats with clinging snow made it appear as if the very ground was moving in ripples as the animals gathered close for warmth and protection.

Tate had stepped down beside the tree line, loosely tethered Shady and with Lobo at his heels, he parted the fog as he moved to a rocky mound to find a target. He dropped to his knee and brought the Sharps to his shoulder, but the low growl of Lobo stopped him. He looked down at the wolf who was standing, facing away from the herd and with lips curling and hackles raised, the big wolf slowly lowered his head, readying to attack.

Tate squinted to see in the gray light and moving fog when several ghostly figures parted the thin blanket of mist as they rode silently toward Tate. He rose from his crouch and faced the group, holding his rifle in the crook of his arm but with the hammer cocked and finger by the trigger guard. As they neared, he saw six native warriors, scowling at what they perceived as an intruder. Tate didn't recognize what tribe but assumed they were Pawnee as he knew they were in their territory. . Richards said the Pawnee had accepted a reservation not far from here and this had all been their hunting territory before.

Tate greeted the men with an "A-ho!" and as one gigged his horse forward, Tate took him for the leader and began to converse in sign. "I am Longbow. I travel with the freighters and am here to take a buffalo for our meat. We go to far cities with goods traded from others."

The leader, a stern-looking warrior whose size was made all the bigger with the sixteen-hand horse he sat on, spoke in English, "I am Big Spotted Horse of the Pitahawirata band of the Pawnee. We too are here for buffalo."

Tate's quick scan of the hunters showed the only rifle was one held by Horse and it was an old trade fusil. He knew that when most tribes accepted the reservation life, they were required as part of the treaty to surrender their rifles and were expected to use just the old fusils or their lances and bows for hunting.

"Hunting in this," Tate said as he motioned with a wave of his hand to the fog and remaining snow, "will be difficult. I have a far shooting rifle," he patted the Sharps in his arm, "I will be glad to shoot some buffalo for you, if your men will help me butcher one for my men." Tate knew an Indian would think it an insult for the white man to think he could do what they could not, and by offering a trade, their pride would be assuaged. He added, "The men I hunt for are anxious to be on the trail, and it would take too long for me to do the work without help."

Big Spotted Horse looked at the white man, trying to judge his intent and when satisfied, swung his leg over the neck of his mount and slid to the ground. He walked forward to look at the rifle but stopped when his eyes dropped to the big wolf beside the man. Tate reached his hand to Lobo's scruff, spoke quietly, "Easy boy, lay down." When the wolf dropped to his belly, the Indian looked to the white man, and slowly approached. Tate gently lowered the hammer and extended the rifle for the big man to examine.

"It is a Sharps, .52 caliber," he dug in his possibles pouch for a paper cartridge to show the man, "this is what it shoots."

The men had been speaking in low tones, and the others had dismounted to see this white man's rifle as well. Spotted Horse returned it to Tate, "I have heard of this. It is called the buffalo gun."

Tate grinned, "That's right. Some have called it that." He looked toward the milling herd and saw they were starting to move away. He moved back to the mound, went to one knee and drew a bead on a sizable cow. He eared back the hammer to a full cock and moved his finger to the thin trigger at the front. He drew in a breath, let part of it out, and slowly squeezed off the shot. The big boom startled the Indians and their ponies with everyone, man and beast, jerking at the blast. Even the snow on the trees behind them slid from the new leaves and fell to the ground. As the Sharps bellowed, it belched a cloud of smoke, made more spectacular by the thin veil of fog, and the targeted cow dropped as if her legs had been pulled out from under her.

The rest of the herd spasmed in surprise, but with no other movement, they didn't spook and run. Tate quickly dropped the lever to open the breech, reloaded and placed a cap on the nipple before bringing the rifle to his shoulder for another shot. This time a young bull was dropped, and Tate again reloaded but motioned for Big Spotted Horse to come beside him and take the shot. The big warrior grinned so wide it appeared the ends of his mouth touched his ears, but he gladly dropped to a knee beside Longbow.

Tate didn't give any instructions but readied the rifle for him. He watched as the man drew the butt to his shoulder and lay his cheek on the stock to take sight. Within barely a breath, the big Sharps boomed and rocked the big man back on his heels. The other warriors couldn't help but laugh at their leader as he handed the rifle back to Tate. A cow had been hit but was staggering, and Tate swiftly reloaded. He made a quick shot, dropped the cow, and with two more blasts from the Sharps, a total of four animals were on the ground.

SEAN LAY along the neck of his appy, fingering the pistol at his waist to reassure himself it was handy. The big horse stretched out into a ground-eating gallop, his nostrils flaring and his mane flying, he loved to run, and man and horse moved as one. Through the wispy blanket of fog, something moved, and Sean slowed his appy. With Stardust, or Dusty as Sean had shortened it, at a trot and Sean standing in his stir-rups, he saw the mounds of snow moving off to his left, and he knew that had to be the buffalo his pa spotted the day before. A few steps further and Sean saw the downed carcass of a big cow and his pa standing beside it, motioning to his son.

"I thought that'd be you, Sean. Hold up and get down, quick now," instructed Tate motioning beyond him. "There's some fellas o'er yonder that might not take it too well if'n ya go ridin' up on 'em real sudden like."

Sean swung his leg over the rump of his horse, and with rifle in hand, dropped to the ground beside his pa. He looked where Tate was looking and saw two warriors approaching. As they neared, Sean followed the lead of his pa and sat the Hawken on its butt beside his leg. Lobo stayed on his belly between the two but watched the warriors with his head lifted and alert.

Tate spoke, "Big Spotted Horse," and put his hand on Sean's shoulder, "this is my son, Bear Chaser."

The big man grinned, looked to the smaller version of the white man, glanced at his rifle and asked, "You do not have a buffalo gun like your father?"

"Not yet, but I hope to soon," answered Sean.

The leader of the warriors drew near and extended his arm in greeting to Sean and the two grasped forearms in friendship. "Your father is a great hunter," and motioned to the dead animals, "but a lousy butcher!" He let out a long belly laugh.

Sean grinned and added, "Yeah, he's always trying to get somebody else to do the bloody work for him."

The warrior looked askance to the white man, then started laughing again, causing all the others to join in. He looked to Tate, "You have a good son."

By the time the butchering was concluding, the sun had burned off the fog, and the rest of the herd had moved on to greener graze away from the disturbance of people, and the wagons were nearing. Richards pulled his wagon near the pile of fresh meat and was somewhat surprised to see Tate and Sean standing beside two Pawnee. He pulled the mules to a stop, and Maggie stood in the seat and started to step down. Once on the ground she boldly approached the men, smiling, and walked to Tate's side.

"Big Spotted Horse, this is my wife, Morning Sky, and that one," he pointed to Sadie standing on the seat of the wagon, "is our daughter, Dancing Owl."

"You have names that are not common among whites. Why is this?" asked Horse.

Tate and Maggie looked at one another and chuckled, "Well, we've gotten our names from different peoples, we've been among the Osage, Comanche, Apache, Ute, Shoshoni, and others. When our young'uns came along, they were named by friends among different people."

He intentionally left out the Arapaho and the Kiowa, knowing the Pawnee had been enemies with both.

Big Spotted Horse grinned, grasped forearms with Tate, and turned away to gather their meat and hides.

WITH OVER THIRTY PEOPLE EATING ON IT, THE BUFFALO DIDN'T last but just over a week. Tate had been kept busy bringing in deer and some small game for the train, and it had proven to be almost a full-time job. The scouting duties required little extra effort, mostly just watching for game or hazards. Most of the Indians that had populated this area had ceded much of their lands to the promise of a reservation and annuity payments of goods and services, most of which were either late or missed entirely. The Kaw, Kickapoo, Shawnee, Potawatomie, Ojibway, Otoe, and others that had been once mighty nations had been decimated by the diseases of the white man and the encroachment of settlers. Tate couldn't help thinking about the great nations to the west and how they were fighting the advancement of the white man, , and he knew it would ultimately be a futile effort. But he understood their plight, especially after seeing the pitiful condition of the tribes in the area they now traveled.

Sean was used to riding out with his pa, but this time Maggie swapped places with the young man, ascribing him the duty of looking after his sister while she rode with her man. They had an early start and followed the north and east side of the Little Blue River. The banks of the river were well shaded with ample hardwoods showing their greenery of spring, and the grasses and brush were strutting their spring colors as well.

Tate reined up near a big burr oak, motioning to Maggie to step down. They ground tied their mounts under the arching branches of the big tree and Tate led the way in a quiet approach to the big bend of the river. They dropped to their knees behind a chokecherry bush and eyed the river bank and sandbar. Four whitetail deer were timidly taking their morning drink from the slow-moving waters, nervously looking around between sips. With hand signs, Tate gave Maggie the choice, and she chose the larger buck showing velvet covered horns that promised to be of considerable size. Tate nodded, motioned to the smaller button buck, and both hunters slowly took their positions behind the tall bush.

Maggie had her alderwood bow and Tate his longbow. Both were skilled with the weapons and often chose them over their rifles to stay in practice. Tate and his father had crafted several longbows as they studied the English and their weapons, and the one he now held was the last longbow they made together. His skill and use of the weapon had given him his name among the natives of the lands he traveled as a young man. It was a powerful weapon and required practiced skill to use. Maggie's bow was patterned after the bows of the Comanche people and was more suited to her size and strength, but it too was deadly in the hands of a proven archer.

As Maggie drew her arrow to full length, she nodded to her husband, and both let fly the missiles of death that whispered to their targets. When the arrows struck, both bucks jumped and the smaller of the two fell on his far shoulder, kicked, and died. Maggie's target turned and started up the bank to follow the fleeing does but stumbled and fell on his face before kicking twice and lying still in death. Both hunters had already nocked arrows but released the draws and stepped from behind the brush to approach the carcasses. The big buck's dying spasm caused it to kick out, startling Maggie, then the animal lay unmoving when she poked his rump with her toe. She breathed easy and looked to Tate, "I'm gonna miss this!" she declared, thinking of the days ahead and the change that lay before them.

Tate turned his face away and lay his bow aside as he reached for his knife and said over his shoulder, "Tryin' not to think about it."

Maggie walked to where the smaller buck lay and found a seat on a large river donie, a water-smoothed stone, and unstrung her bow and sat quietly as Tate worked. She just wanted to be near her man, conversation wasn't necessary, just the nearness. Her thoughts went to the difficult decision that had brought them to this place and would all too soon be the cause of their parting. The sacrifices parents made for their children often brought heartache and even hardship, but the love of a mother or father for their children knew no limits.

"Here, you carry my bow while I wrangle these deer up to that tree yonder. We'll hang 'em so Richards'll see 'em and throw 'em on the wagon. But unless I miss my guess, Sean'll prob'ly see 'em 'fore Richards."

"I don't doubt that. That man is either talking his head off or mumbling to himself in one of his sullen moods. He is hard to understand, that man is. I don't know how he's managed to stay alive. I think all he ever sees is the backsides of those mules!" declared Maggie, laughing..

As Tate followed Maggie up the riverbank, carrying the carcass of the smaller buck across his shoulders, he said,

"That man sees more'n you think he does. And he knows his business; he's been doin' it for most of a decade now." They were nearing the big oak when Tate hissed and dropped to his knee, lowering the buck to the ground. Maggie followed his example and looked in the direction he was staring. Lobo was at his side and in a crouch, growling as he looked beyond the trees.

It was a group of men, white men, traveling in what appeared to be a military formation. But they did not have uniforms of any kind, all were attired in homespun or the like, yet all carried rifles over the pommels of their saddles.

"Who do you s'pose they are?" whispered Maggie. The men were about a hundred yards from the tree line, moving at a walk, no hurry but determined in their manner.

"I dunno, but for that many to be armed and on the move, they ain't huntin' that's for sure. Maybe a posse or sump'in like that from some town hereabouts."

They watched as the men moved into the thicker trees near the confluence of the Big Blue and Little Blue rivers, where Tate had been told was the crossing the wagons would take to reach the flats beyond the Big Blue.. The column of men showed themselves again on the far bank of the river and turned south to apparently follow the larger stream. Tate and Maggie waited until the men were well away and out of sight before they went to their horses.

"You wait here while I go get the other'n but be watchful."

Maggie nodded her head and went to her buckskin to tighten the cinch and be ready to move out. Tate hastened to the second carcass and dragged the larger animal to the tree where the horses stood.. "I'm thinkin' we might oughta either go back to the wagons or wait for 'em here. Don't know what that bunch mighta been up to but we sure don't want the wagons runnin' into any ambush."

Maggie answered, "Won't hafta go back. Lookee yonder!"

and motioned with her head and pointed to the approaching wagons. .

"They musta got an early start, that's good."

When the wagons approached, Sadie was standing in the seat of the lead wagon driven by John Richards and waving at her folks. Maggie waved back, smiling at the sight of her little girl and her long red curls bouncing with her exuberance. Sean road his appy alongside the wagon and lifted his head, trying to show his indifference at the sight of his ma and pa. But his impatience got the better of him, and he clucked to his stallion, and the two trotted to the trees to see the waiting deer carcasses. When the lead wagon pulled up, Tate walked to the side and looked up at Richards, "Saw a bunch o' men, looked kinda military like, ridin' in a column, all of 'em armed and carryin' their rifles o'er their pommels, but no uniforms or nothin'. Don't know what to make of 'em."

"Didja see any red on 'em, like on their pants legs?" asked Richards.

"No, no, don't reckon. Nothin' like that. Why?"

"How long ago did they pass?"

"Less'n a quarter hour. What'chu thinkin'?" asked Tate, his curiosity piqued.

Richards stepped down from the wagon, wrapping the leads around the brake handle and motioned to the wagons behind to stop for a break.. He looked to Tate, "Guess I need to fill you in on a couple things. Let's have some coffee, and I'll give you a quick eddication." He went to the back of the wagon and brought out the coffee pot and the bag of Arbuckles.

The teamsters and helpers didn't hesitate to make their own fires and put on the coffee as Richards set the example, and Tate, Maggie, and a few others gave an assist with firewood and a couple of grey cottonwood logs for seats. When

Tate and Richards had their cups of hot brew, the wagon leader sat on the ground, stretched out his legs and leaned back against the log to begin his monologue.

"We are now in Bloody Kansas. It's been this way for a few years now an' most folks don't see it changin' anytime soon. Ya see, when they did the Kansas-Nebraska Act that made these two territories, slavery was outlawed in 'em. But ever since that fella, Fremont, lost to Buchanan," he paused when Tate held up his hand to stop him..

"What? Fremont? John Fremont? The one they called Pathfinder?" asked the surprised Tate.

"Yeah, that's the one. Why?"

"Pathfinder! That man couldn't find his way out of a one-room cabin! Are you tellin' me that he was in that whatever it was an' wantin' to be the president?"

Richards chuckled, "Sounds to me like you had a run-in with the man. That right?"

Tate shook his head, "You could say that. But never mind that, go on with what you were sayin' 'bout the slavery issue."

"Well, there's been an ongoin' argument 'mong most folks 'bout whether there oughta be slavery or not. An' with the possibility of Kansas and Nebraska comin' into the union, it would upset the balance of pro-slavery and free states, so that's kinda been what they been fightin' about hereabouts. The Border Ruffians as they're called, are wantin' Kansas to be a slave state, an' the Jayhawkers or Red Legs are for a free state. Trouble is, most of 'em ain't even from Kansas, they come in from Missoura an' other places east an' they been causin' a ruckus for a few years now. Far as I'm concerned, it's all a bunch o' nonsense, but I'm thinkin' it's gonna get a whole lot worse 'fore it gets any better."

"What'chu mean worse?"

"Wal, lot'sa folks are thinkin' it's gonna break out into an all-out war. There's a couple politicians been carryin' on, uh, oh yeah, a senator name o' Stephen Douglas and a right popular fella named Abraham Lincoln. And of course, there's John Brown. He was one o' them that was stirrin' things up round 'chere and led some raids hereabouts."

"So, I reckon that means we could have a run-in with just 'bout anybody," surmised Tate.

"Ummhumm, that's 'bout it. So, as you're scoutin' out there, just keep in mind, we ain't involved in any o' the fight. We just wanna get our wagons to St. Louie. So, if'n you run into any of 'em, just be almighty cautious, but don't start nothin'."

Tate nodded his head, understanding, and tossed the dregs of the coffee at the embers of the fire. He turned to Maggie, "It's prob'ly best if you an' Sadie stay back with the wagons. I might take Sean with me, but I reckon we'll just have to tread lightly 'till we're further into Missouri."

He stood, looked down to Richards, "That river crossin' you talked about up here at the confluence of these two rivers is where them fellas crossed over. So, after we cross, we'll be goin' south along the Big Blue?"

"That's right. The trail will take us a little away from the river then it's 'bout a 'nother day or two 'till we reach the Kansas River. There's a ferry there where we'll cross to the south side o' the Kansas; then we go east to Missouri!"

Tate nodded his head, motioned to Sean and gave Lobo a hand signal, and headed to his horse. Maggie followed at his side, and when he was ready to mount up, they embraced, and she leaned back and said, "You be careful, an' take care of our son!"

Tate ducked his head, stubbed his toe in the dirt, "Aw, he'll prob'ly be takin' care of me. You just try to keep yourself and Sadie outta trouble. Just to be on the safe side, keep your Sharps in the wagon box with you."

"Always do!" she said as she tiptoed to give her man a kiss.

CHAPTER FOUR
JAYHAWKERS

LATE AFTERNOON ON THE SECOND DAY AFTER THE BLUE RIVER crossing, Tate and Sean sat in their saddles, leaning on the pommels, staring at the ferry making its way across the sandy-bottomed Kansas River. It was Sean's first sighting of any boat bigger than an Indian birchbark canoe, and he stared agape as the men worked the rope to move the ferry across the water. The trees were at their back, and they crossed the roadway to the ferry ramp and tethered their horses in front of the cabin that served as the ferryman's home. The sign on the side read, *Smith/Kennedy Ferry, Wagon and team, $1.25, Horses .15, men .10, women and children .05.*

As Tate looked at the sign a man came from the cabin, scowling at the visitor. . "Just you two an' the horses, fifty cent! Ferry'll be back in a couple minutes, might as well sit a spell. Come fer, have ye?"

Tate eyed the man wearing high water britches, bare-footed, galluses over bare shoulders with one thumb stretching them away from his chest and the other hand holding a smoldering corn-cob pipe. Tate answered, "Not so far today, but we started out from the Rockies."

The man's eyebrows lifted as he stuck the pipe in one corner of his mouth, freeing his second thumb to balance his galluses pulling them both away from his hairy chest. "Ye ain't carryin' much fer comin' so fer."

"It's in the wagons comin'."

"Wagons eh? How many? What they carryin'? Mules or horses?"

Tate had to wait until the man took a breath before attempting to answer his questions, "Four schooners, twelve freighters, hides and trade stuff, mules and a few horses."

The man's eyebrows lifted again, and the greed showed in his brightened eyes as he was obviously counting the fares. He turned his face to the sky to guess the remaining daylight, "Might get 'em all acrost 'fore dark, mebbe not, but we can still cross with the lanterns blazin'."

Tate looked to Sean, "Son, what will that come to for all the wagons?"

Sean grinned, knowing his pa never missed an opportunity to put Sean's learning to practice, "Sixteen wagons at a dollar and a quarter comes out to an even twenty dollars. But I'm sure the good ferryman will be glad to give us a discount for the large number and let us cross for, oh, say, sixteen dollars."

"Sixteen dollars!!" shouted the man, stepping from the stoop in front of the cabin, "Now see here younker, I ain't gonna give no discount like that! I got 'spenses! Twenty dollars it is!"

Sean looked to his pa seriously, "Well, Pa, guess you were right. We'll hafta go downstream to the Pappan ferry after all. Their ferry is bigger an' can prob'ly get us across faster anyway." He reached for the reins laying on Dusty's neck and glanced at the ferryman.

"Now, hold on thar! Alright, alright, I'll do it fer nineteen dollars, that's savin' you a whole dollar."

"Not good enough. We'll do it for eighteen or not at all," answered Sean, lifting his foot toward the stirrup.

"Consarn it you whippersnapper you! Eighteen dollars," grumbled the ferryman as he started toward the returning ferry. He hollered over his shoulder, "Ya better git 'em here in a hurry, time's a'wastin'!"

Tate waved his hand toward the roadway, pointing out the approaching wagons, and turned back to his son, grinning. He nodded his head as he chuckled and stepped back aboard Shady to deliver the terms to Richards. Sean sat on the edge of the stoop, stroking Lobo's scruff and watching the unloading of the ferry.

Tate and Sean crossed with the first wagon driven by John Richards and carrying Maggie and Sadie. Richards chose to stay and direct the wagons as they crossed and asked Tate to take the wagon to the bottoms to the west of the old Baptist Mission and set up camp. Maggie had taken to cooking for the drivers of the four wagons, while the teamsters had their own cook to tend to the meals for the men of the twelve freighters. She corralled Sean into helping and put Tate to work slicing steaks from the fresh haunch of venison taken that morning.

By the time the meal was ready, John Richards ambled up to the fire looking a little on the side of bedraggled. He plopped himself down on a ladder-back chair and accepted a full plate from Maggie, who commented, "You look like you're about done in, maybe you should think about resting up a mite."

He pulled the coffee cup toward him, bent his head to take a deep drought, and answered, "Yup, I think we'll hold up here a day or so, tend to some repairs and let the animals get some rest. From here to St. Louis is 'bout three weeks, mebbe a little more, so we're on the downhill side."

Tate looked at the man, "Looks to me like you've got somethin' else botherin' you. What is it?"

The hungry men barely paused in their eating, but Richards answered, "I was talkin' to one o' the ferrymen. He said they been havin' more'n more trouble from the Jayhawkers an' Ruffians. Nothin' real bad, but dependin' on which bunch, they been makin' it hard on travelers. Seems some have been bringin' in weapons an' such for this fightin' that's goin' on."

"Just exactly how they been makin' it hard?" asked Tate.

"They stop the wagons an' wanna search 'em. Then they take whatever they want and destroy most of what's left."

"Sounds more like thieves an' outlaws to me. You're not gonna stand for that are ya?"

"After what we been through to get this far? Ha! These farmboys an' their pups don't know what they'll be up against!"

Tate relaxed and sat back, bringing his coffee cup to his mouth as he chuckled at Richards' response. It just was not in Tate's nature to back down from a fight and when would-be toughs tried to take advantage of others, it just got his hackles up. Never one to look for a fight, there just wasn't any back-up in him. He had faced grizzly bears, mountains lions, and any number of conflicts with different warring Indian bands, and to think he would come to what others called civilization and let anyone make him take water, no sir.

IT WAS late morning on the third day after their rest break in the bottoms below the Kansas or Kaw River crossing when Tate and Sean spotted a sizeable group of riders coming from the east. Although ahead of the wagons, Richards had asked Tate to stay within sight just in case they did happen upon one of the talked about bands of raiders. Tate nudged Sean's horse to the edge of the road and motioned for him to get into the trees. "You take cover yonder, stay in the saddle, but have your rifle ready." Sean nodded and moved away. The two were at a slight bend in the road, and Tate believed they had not been seen. He sidestepped Shady to the middle and crosswise of the road, lay his Sharps across his pommel and with his left shoulder facing the riders, he waited.

Led by two men in the front, the band of about a dozen all appeared a little slovenly, but each man had a rifle either sitting butt down on their leg, across the pommel, or hanging loosely at their sides. It was evident they were looking for trouble. Both leaders moved towards Tate, side by side, but one gigged his horse forward to come alongside Tate,, close enough to be within arms-length..

The leader had thin whiskers, a few snaggly tobacco-stained teeth, , and a grin that wrinkled his nose as he sneered at Tate. "Wal, what have we here? You'n yore buck-skins, whatchu tryin' to be, a mountain man 'er sumpin'?"

Tate looked the man over, and without turning his head gave the second man the same Looking back at the speaker, "I don't have to *try* to be anything, I am what I am, and that's more'n I can say for some folks."

The speaker grinned and turned back to his friend, "Whoooeeee, we got us a smart one hyar!" He looked back to Tate, "Now, hows about you gittin' outta our way, we got us some wagons to tend to!" nodding his head toward the approaching train. He cocked the hammer on his rifle and started to lift it, but Tate suddenly rammed the muzzle of the big Sharps into the leader's throat, knocking him from his saddle. Tate dug heels to Shady who leaped forward and rammed the shoulder of the second man's horse just as that man was fumbling for his rifle both went to the ground. Tate raised his Sharps toward the rest of the group and hollered,

"Now if any of you think you wanna shake hands with the devil hisself, just try raising your rifle!"

A big scruffy man looked at Tate and hollered to his friends, "He's only one! Let's get him!"

Suddenly Sean's rifle roared from the trees, shattering the stock of one man's rifle, but Tate did not turn to look, keeping his Sharps leveled towards the group. "What's that you were sayin' big man?"

"Uh, uh, nothin', I guess."

The entire group was restless, horses moving about, some wanting to skedaddle, but Tate stopped them, "Now, all of you, drop your rifles to the ground, NOW!" he shook his rifle to emphasize his command. One man tossed his rifle to the grass at the edge of the road, then another, and soon all were free of their weapons. Tate knew many of them probably had handguns or other weapons, but he had them cowered. He heard Sean's horse come from the trees and the trace chains of the approaching wagons.

Richards voice came from behind him, "We've got 'em covered, Tate." What Tate could not see was the freighter with six men and their rifles covering the raiders, but the wide eyes of the would-be bandits showed their fear.

Tate spoke, "Now, you fellas best high-tail it outta here, and," he raised his voice, "don't all of you go in the same direction! Now GIT!" He fired his Sharps over their heads, and the big boom of the buffalo gun spooked the horses into action, with one plow horse trying to buck but the big farmer pulled the horse's chin to his chest and stopped his attempts . Tate turned enough to see the two leaders scramble aboard their horses and kick them into a run to catch their friends.

Tate looked to Sean with a questioning expression, and Sean just pointed to the ground and the shattered stock of a rifle. "He tried to pick it up when he was behind you. I convinced him otherwise."

Tate grinned, pride showing in his eyes, "Thanks son. I was countin' on you keepin' me outta trouble."

"That's gettin' to be a full-time job!"

CHAPTER FIVE
MISSOURI

MISSOURI WAS A LEARNING EXPERIENCE FOR SEAN, WITH TATE teaching and quizzing him all the way about the different trees, bushes, birds and other animals unique to the country-side. He was most impressed with a flying squirrel that crossed overhead when the trail cut between two towering oaks. He made a double take and looked to his pa, "What was that?"

Tate chuckled as he answered, "That was what they call a flying squirrel."

"Did it have wings?" asked a flabbergasted Sean, searching the upper branches for another glimpse of the soaring furball.

"No, not really, and they don't fly, they kinda glide. It's the loose skin between their legs that they spread out and glide from one tree to the other."

"Well, 'tween squirrels that fly, giant rats that live in trees, what'd you call 'em, Possums? And frogs big 'nuff to eat, this is mighty strange country."

Tate laughed with his son, "Son, you'll find that every part of the country, actually the world, has its own special features. Sometimes it's just the land and the vegetation, but it's often the animals as well."

"Well, what other strange creatures are we gonna see?"

"Oh, I dunno, guess we'll just hafta wait and see, ya reckon?"

They were three days out of Jefferson City, the capital of Missouri, , and since entering the state, their travel had been without incident. But the eyes of Sean were certainly getting their fill as he surveyed the different terrain.

"So, whatcha think of this part of the world?" asked Tate giving a wide sweep of his hand.

"Well, it sure is different. All these leafy trees, the woods are too thick to go through, and all these people! And I ain't used to not bein' able to see very far. We get up on a bit of a rise an' all we can see is more trees! An' it seems like every place where there ain't trees, there's farms! Sure are a lot of people!"

"Well, you're right about that, an' the closer we get to St. Louis, the more people we see. Lookee yonder," Tate motioned with a head nod toward a wide valley, "farms as far as you can see an' the only thing between 'em is a hedgerow or a rock wall. When they're livin' that close together you gotta be careful when you're out huntin', cuz ya' might hit your neighbor!"

"Was it like this when you lived here before, Pa?"

"Where we lived was about a week's ride south of here, and it wasn't quite like this then, but who knows, could be now."

"Is this why so many wagon trains are headin' out west? I mean, cuz there's so many folks an' all."

"That's part of it, Sean. But a lot of 'em head west cuz they think they're gonna find a lotta free land, and it'll be easier livin' and some of 'em think they're gonna strike it rich in the gold fields."

"Do they? Strike it rich, I mean," asked the youngster.

"Well, from what I hear, there have been a few of 'em hit paydirt out in California country. But for everyone that makes a strike, there's probably a hundred that die tryin'. And then there's the others that give up and go back to farmin' or whatever they left behind. What most of 'em don't realize is that wherever they go, there they are."

Sean frowned, not understanding what his pa meant and shook his head before asking, "Wherever they go, there they are? What's that mean?"

"Well son, some folks are wantin' somethin' for nuthin'. They're not willing to put in the work it takes to make whatever they're doin' successful. Like farming. To be successful at farming requires a lot of hard work, clearing the land, plowing, planting, and everything that goes with it, every bit of it hard work. But for those that like the land and are willing to work, it's an honorable life and a good life. But the man that fails at farming here," motioning with his hand to the fertile green fields, "is going to be the same man across the Rockies. Wherever he goes, there he is. And if he's not willing to do the work here to succeed, he won't do it anywhere, and he'll still fail. Because he's the problem and he won't admit it and change.

"That's why he'll pack up his family and move clear across country, griping all the way, and think life'll be easier somewhere else. But until he realizes he has to work just as hard wherever he is and becomes willing to do the work, he's still gonna fail."

"Is that always what happens, Pa?"

"The principle's the same, but some can change what they're doing. For example, a farmer can become a miner and do well, or a storekeeper can become a trapper and succeed. But whether they change jobs or locations, they're still gonna hafta put in the work to make a success. It's those that want something for nothing that become the outlaws and thieves and try to take what they want from others."

Sean was silent and thoughtful for a stretch and leaned forward to rest his arm on the pommel, "So, is that why there's so many graves along the Oregon trail?"

"That's part of it. And the sad part is when families have to suffer for the doin' of it. The wives and children that stand by the man, even though they know he's not what he should be, are the ones that pay the highest price. But, sometimes, it's the love of a good woman that gets the man to straighten up and do right. Just remember, anyone can change, both for the good and the bad."

They had ridden just a few miles when another wide valley showed a large and impressive farm. The main house was a sizable structure with a touch of southern architecture with four massive white columns across the front. Several other buildings peeked from the trees to the side of the big house, and a large barn showed itself behind the white building. Large fields spread out in front of the main house, and several teams were at work. i.

Sean and Tate reined up to look, stepping down from their horses to give them a drink in the small spring-fed pool beneath a big oak. They let the horses graze as they sat on a slight knoll and watched the workers in the fields beyond. Sean let a frown wrinkle his forehead as he pointed, "Those fields have already been planted and are showin' green, so what're the teams doin'?"

"I think that's what they call a harrow. They use it to plow under the weeds between the rows of the plants. I'm not sure what the plants are, maybe tobacco."

"You see that every one of those teams is driven by a negro? Are they slaves?"

"Probably. See that man on the horse at the edge of the field? He's what they call an overseer, he's the boss and makes sure the work is done the way he wants."

Sean scowled as he looked, "Pa, the way I see it, that ain't no different than when the Indians take captives and make them do the work around the camp. I don't think that's right."

"I'd have to agree with your son. And the question of slavery is what's causin' a lot of these problems we run into, like that bunch of Jayhawkers that tried to take the wagons. There's lotsa folks that think slavery should be outlawed and others, probably like that farmer down there, that want to keep it."

"But they're still people, Pa! Just cuz their skin's a different color don't mean nothin'. We seen lotsa people that are different from us, but they're still people. Don't the Bible say somethin' 'bout it?"

Tate dropped his head, "With all the 'one another's' in the scripture, there is never a qualifier. When God says *Love one another as I have loved you.* He doesn't say to just love those that look like you, He says 'one another.' Now, He doesn't say there shouldn't be any slavery, because, in the Old Testament, there was.. But neither does He condone it. It's kinda hard to fulfill the 'one another' part if the other one is your slave."

Sean stood, readying to leave, and looked to his pa as they mounted. "That's another reason I like the mountains better. I don't think I could be around this," he motioned to the field with the slaves, "and not do somethin' about it."

As they neared the city, farms covered the land with nothing to divide them but fences or hedgerows. Houses were often within throwing distance of one another, and the roadway was crowded with buggies, wagons, and horsemen. Groups of travelers, many of them negroes, went on foot with bags over their shoulders. On the south side of the road, a large Victorian style home gleamed white and stood proudly, showing its grandeur. A simple sign at the roadway leading to the structure read *'Finney's Inn'.*

Tate reined up, pointing, "This must be the place John spoke about. Let's go have a looksee. The wagons'll be along shortly."

Sean asked, "You mean we're here?"

Tate laughed at his son, "Where else could we be besides here?"

"Ah Pa, you know what I mean. Is there where we'll be stayin'?"

"That depends, son, we'll have to make sure they have room for us. Richards said this is the best place, near enough to town but far enough out to be away from things."

As they tethered their horses at the hitch rail, Tate looked at the big house. A wide veranda swept across the front and down the right side. What appeared as a tower was at the left end and stood three stories high. A balcony extended from the second floor over the veranda and the peak of the roof showed a window that might be the third floor or an attic. It was a massive house but very well kept with the clapboard siding showing fresh white paint. The windows on the first story extended from the floor to the ceiling of the veranda. The wide stairs led to the front double doors, one of which stood open to invite visitors in..

Once inside, Tate stopped to look at the wide staircase that rose to a landing and split to both sides of the second level. The wide entryway had a standing desk with an open register and a quill pen atop, but no one was present. Tate suddenly felt very conscious of his rough appearance with well-worn buckskins, moccasins, and a floppy felt hat that he quickly doffed. He motioned to Sean to do the same, and both stood waiting as they heard the click of heels on the floor approaching.

"May I help you, gentlemen?" The voice came from an immaculately attired matronly woman who stepped behind the standing desk. A waft of perfume followed her, and she stood waiting for a response.

"Uh, yes ma'am. We need a couple rooms," answered Tate, haltingly.

"For the two of you?" asked the woman, looking down at her register and with a dubious expression that made Tate wonder at her manner.

"Uh, no, well, yes. It's for my wife and daughter and me an' muh son, here."

The woman lifted her eyes to the man and asked, "Will they join you soon?"

"Yes ma'am. They'll be with the wagons. Mr. Richards said this would be the best place for us to stay."

"Mr. Richards? Would that be John Richards, the trader?" asked the woman, her tense expression relaxing just a mite.

"Yes ma'am. We just came in from the west. Been travelin' quite some time and my missus is anxious to have a hot bath. You do have baths don't you?"

"Will you be staying long? Mr. . . uh, Mr. ?"

"Not rightly sure ma'am. Maggie, that's my wife, and Sadie, my daughter, will be staying what you might call long-term. Not too sure 'bout me'n the boy."

"I see."

"No ma'am, I don't think you do. You see ma'am, Sadie's getting to an age she needs to have a proper education, not that my wife couldn't do that, but she's a very intelligent young lady, and we believe it best if she gets the best education possible."

The woman nodded her head and asked, "And your name sir?" she held the quill pen over the register waiting.

"Saint, Tate Saint. This is my son Sean."

The woman's eyes lifted to the buckskin-clad man and asked, "Is Saint short for something else?"

"Uh, why yes, yes, it is, I just haven't used it in so long, purt near forgot. My full name is Tatum St. Michael."

The woman looked at Tate long and hard, took a deep breath and leaned on the desk as she wrote the name in the register. She took two keys from a small drawer, handed them to Tate and said, "There's a barn in the back. You may put your animals in any empty stall or the corral behind the barn. There's hay in the mow. When you return, these keys are for the two rooms at the front of the house on the second floor. When your wife arrives, we will prepare a bath for her." She looked at Tate and Sean, "And if anyone else would like one we will do the same. Now, will that be in coin or currency?"

Tate detected something behind the woman's manner but couldn't make it out and passed it off to her business as an innkeeper. He reached into a pouch hanging inside his belted britches and placed two twenty-dollar gold pieces on the desk.

The woman lifted her wide eyes to the man, "Oh, my. That's too much, Mr. St. Michaels."

"Just keep an account and when you need more, let me know."

"Yessir. Dinner will be served in the dining room," she motioned to her right, "at six."

"Thank you ma'am, and about that bath, we both would like one, thank you."

Tate turned back to the door, Sean at his heels, and stepped to the veranda and drew in a deep breath. He shook his head, "Nope, sure not like the mountains!" He descended the steps, and both men grabbed the reins to lead their horses to the barn. With Lobo following at their heels, both were thinking about what this 'adventure' was going to bring and neither man, young or old, was anxious to spend any more time than necessary in this 'civilization.'

Mrs. Finney stood beside her chair at the head of the long table. She wore a bright blue dress with a tiered skirt. The long-pointed bodice was trimmed with horizontal bands of ruching over a chemise. Her bare shoulders accented the white lace, and her dark hair with touches of grey framed an attractive face. She smiled at her guests as they came to the table to stand behind their chairs. Tate and Sean were in their newest buckskins with beading that fell from the shoulders and accented their broad physiques.

The long table seated twelve and Tate and Sean were seated to the immediate left of their hostess, leaving chairs for Maggie and Sadie. Tate casually looked at the other guests, three men, and two women. The couple across the table from Tate were older, both sporting white hair and were distinguished looking. The woman seemed to look down her nose at the buckskin-clad men opposite her, but Tate was not concerned with her opinion or attitude. Next to them was the only other woman, a young lady in a simple print dress that appeared quite self-conscious and even bashful. Two men, well attired in the fashion of gentlemen, also appeared to be brothers with their similar appearances.

The tapping of heels on the hardwood floor made Tate turn and look to see Maggie as she seemed to float into the room. She wore a simple green satin dress with laced short sleeves over a linen chemise, and tiny rose-colored tassels adorned the peaks of her shoulders. Her white shoulders contrasted with her tanned face and neck and a parade of freckles marched across her chest. Her long red hair hung in curls to her shoulders, and she put a small hanky to her mouth to keep from laughing at the expression on her husband's face.

Tate stood frozen as he looked at Maggie, his eyes following her every step as she passed behind him to stand by her chair next to her man. Sadie walked quietly and shyly to the side of Sean, wearing a white lacy dress with a crinoline petticoat. Her darker red hair was also in curls, and she blushed when Sean looked at his sister, mouth agape in surprise. Maggie whispered to Tate, "Mrs. Finney had these dresses for us. Aren't they pretty?" Before he could respond with anything other than a head nod, their hostess spoke.

"Well, Mr. McGillicutty, would you do us the honor and ask the Lord's blessing on our meal?" Mrs. Finney was looking to the elderly gentleman to her right and waited for an answer.

"Certainly, Mrs. Finney." He looked around the table to each of the other guests and said, "Let us pray." He had a very somber tone and resonant voice and he spoke in a manner to emphasize what he thought was his spirituality. He began, "Our most gracious Heavenly Father, . . . " and continued with a lengthy prayer mentioning many things that had little to do with their meal. When he finally closed with, ". . . and we thank you. Aaaaamen!"

Mrs. Finney pulled out her chair and seated herself,

setting the example for the others. Tate pulled out Maggie's chair and seated her and Sean followed his example for Sadie. During the table conversation, it was revealed that Mr. McGillicutty was a retired minister, Miss Dinwoody was a student at St. Louis University pursuing her degree to become a teacher, and the brothers Whitcomb were employed in businesses downtown. When the attention was turned to the Saint's, Mrs. Finney asked, "Mr. Saint Michaels, that is an unusual name, not one often heard. Do you know the history of your name?"

"Actually Mrs. Finney, I've never used the full name of Saint Michaels, my father dropped the Michaels part when he came as a young man from Saint Michaels Isle, a part of the Isle of Man off the coast of England. He thought the full name sounded a little too stuffy and preferred the shortened version of Saint."

Mrs. Finney nodded her head, "I see. Are your parents still living?"

"No, ma'am. My mother passed. She nursed several of the people in the Osage Village near Cape Girardeau and was taken by the pox. My father was a school teacher, and we went to Springfield after Mother passed, but he was shot by a crooked cardsharp."

"And how long ago was that?"

"I had just turned fifteen at the time, ma'am. So, it was a considerable time."

"I'm sorry to hear that. What was your father's name?"

Tate frowned a little at the questioning of the woman. In the west, no one pried into another's past and personal questions were considered rude and even insulting. But thinking there was no harm in answering the curious woman, Tate responded, "My father's name was Johnathan, and my Mother was Ellie or Eleanor."

Mrs. Finney gave a quick gasp but brought her hanky to

her mouth to hide her surprise and asked, "And did you know your Mother's maiden name?"

Tate frowned, thinking this woman was too inquisitive and asked, "I don't understand ma'am. Where we come from, personal questions of this manner are considered rude and uncalled for, so I can't help but wonder why you're so interested."

"Please bear with me a moment longer. Your mother's maiden name?"

"Patterson, ma'am. Her name was Eleanor Patterson."

"Did she ever speak of a sister named LaVinia?"

Tate's brow furrowed, and his lips tightened as he looked at this persistent woman, "I only recall her speaking of one sister she called Vinny."

"I am LaVinia, Vinny, Patterson. Your mother's sister!" proclaimed the smiling hostess with tear filled eyes.

A collective gasp came from most of the group at the table, and Tate stared open-mouthed at the woman. He looked long and hard and as he slowly began to see his mother in the face of this woman, he let a smile paint his face.

"I never thought I'd ever see anyone from my family ever again." He shook his head, fumbling with nervous fingers at the tableware, and finally scooted back his chair and went to the woman. She stood and met him with open arms, and they hugged, pulling apart to look at one another and hugged again. Everyone sat silent as the two shared a special moment until Tate returned to his chair and grabbed a linen napkin to dab the tears in his eyes. Maggie leaned over and hugged her man, smiling happily at the reunion.

Vinny smiled at the man with his head bowed slightly, the red of embarrassment showing at his collar, "The last time I saw you, you were only this high," she held her hand to her side about three feet high. "And you were so full of energy and mischief." She smiled and laughed at the thought. She looked to Maggie, "Is he still like that?"

Maggie smiled and looked at Tate, "Yes he is, but it's good mischief, most of the time."

As the others excused themselves from the table, the Saints and their new-found aunt spent the rest of the evening getting acquainted. As the evening drew to a close, Vinny said, "I am so happy you are all here. And if you," nodding her head toward Maggie, "and the little one would like, I would love to have you stay with me for as long as you like. After all, we are family!"

As Tate and Maggie lay in what Tate thought was an uncomfortably soft feather bed and the heavy quilt at their feet, he felt a little restless. "I feel like I've been caught in a avalanche or sumpin'," he kicked at the quilt and flipped back the spread, "Whooeee!"

Maggie giggled at her husband's antics and said, "You just miss the smell of pines, the cold fresh mountain air, the crackle of the cicadas, and the nightbird's call."

"Don'tchu?"

"Well, yes, but this is nice too. Have you ever felt something so soft?"

Tate grinned as he rolled to his side to look into the green eyes of his sweetheart, and answered, "Oh, I can think of something even better!" He grinned as he lay his arm across her waist. Maggie stretched up to kiss her man as he pulled her close.

CHAPTER SEVEN
SHOPPING

VINNY AND HER HOUSEMAID SET A SUMPTUOUS TABLE FOR breakfast. She shared with Tate and Maggie that her helper had been an indentured servant who came from Ireland after the potato famine of '45. Many families were broken by it and the typhoid and cholera epidemics that followed. Mary was from Cashel, County Tipperary, and had lost her mother and father when they were separated in the poorhouses or workhouses and fell to the epidemics. One of the rulers of Ireland, Earl Grey, developed a program for many of the young orphans to be shipped to Australia and the new world of America as indentured servants.

"But Mary is no longer indentured, and she has become like a daughter to me, and she has been a great help these last few years," explained Vinny. "I have seen to her education, but she doesn't take well to the study for more. She is more suited for the work here, and I'm happy to have her, but she's a lovely lass and catches the eye of many a man."

By her appearance, Mary could have been a younger sister to Maggie: long red hair, freckles, and deep green eyes. Always busy, Mary enjoyed her work and sought to please her mistress. As she tended to the table, Tate noticed the brothers Whitcomb would often glance her way, but nothing untoward was happening.

Tate looked to the brothers, "You fellas said you worked in businesses downtown, may I ask what type of business?"

Horace Whitcomb, the older brother, responded, "Certainly. I work at the Western Emporium for Mssrs. Dimick and Company. My brother manages the store of Mr. Hjorring where they have a wide assortment of clothing for both men and women."

"And the Western Emporium, what do they have?"

"Anything and everything for the adventurer. From every manner of weaponry, rifles, shotguns, pistols, knives, to fishing tackle, and more. All the paraphernalia of the sportsman. And we employ twenty-seven gunsmiths that build or modify all manner of firearms."

Tate grinned, "That sounds like my kinda store!"

Henry Whitcomb interjected, "Perhaps you would like to purview our clothing line for yourself or your missus? We are known as the most fashionable haberdasher in town."

"Well, I'm sure my wife will spend some time there, but unless you carry buckskins . . . " he grinned at the mental image of himself in the accouterments of a fashionable gentleman of the city, "I probably won't be visiting there."

VINNY INSISTED they take her carriage into town to do their shopping and Maggie insisted she join them, to which she gladly acquiesced. "And I have just the dressmaker for you and Sadie, she can do such wonders with material!"

Tate looked to Sean and whispered, "We'll find all the wonders we need in the Emporium!" Sean grinned at his pa and nodded his head enthusiastically. Tate had promised his son a new rifle to replace his well-used Hawken, but he had been careful not to specify just what he might be getting. In his campfire conversations with John Richards and some of the others, he learned there had been considerable advancement in the firearms, and he was anxious to see if the Dimick store was stocked as well as Horace Whitcomb had implied.

Finney's Inn was to the southwest of St. Louis and the shoppers traveled into the city on Carondelet Road to the heart of the business district on Market Street. As they rode along, the youngsters were amazed at the buildings and the people, and although they tried not to show it as much, Tate and Maggie were equally surprised. Although he had been in St. Louis about fifteen years before, much had changed, and the growth was astounding to the family from the mountains. Vinney watched them all, thrilled at their excitement, and willingly answered their questions about the city.

As they neared the business district, Tate asked, "Could we make a stop at the Boatmen's Bank first? I have a little business to tend to if you don't mind?"

Vinny was somewhat startled at her nephew but readily agreed to the stop, which piqued her curiosity considerably. She was well known in the bank, having done business with them for many years. Her husband had been employed there before he bought their property and home where Vinny now had her Inn.

As they pulled up before the stately building, Tate stepped down and assisted the ladies as they exited the carriage. "You two just wait right here for us, we won't be too long," instructed Tate as he looked to the youngsters. He turned to accompany the ladies into the bank, opening the wide door for them and followed them into the cavernous interior. A man with spectacles resting on the end of his nose greeted them, giving Tate a snobbish once-over and quickly turning his attention to Mrs. Finney..

"Mrs. Finney, what a pleasure to see you this morning. How may we help you?" asked the clerk.

"My nephew, Tate, has some business here he needs to tend to if you would be so kind as to assist him?" she held her open palm at her shoulder, signifying Tate.

The clerk turned toward him eyeing his buckskins, and extended his smooth white hand and said, "I am Archibald Jenkins, I am the assistant to the president, Mr. J. N. Taylor. How may I help you?"

Tate looked at the portly man, accepted his offered handshake and squeezed a little more than usual just to watch the man wince, and answered, "My name is Tate Saint, and my business would be with Mr. Taylor."

"Hummph, Mr. Taylor is busy, and I'm certain I can take care of whatever business you have."

"No, I don't think you can. Besides, my business is my business and between me and Mr. Taylor. So, lead the way please."

"But, but . . . " stammered the clerk, but the wave of Tate's hand sent him on his way toward the president's office. He motioned for Tate to wait and stepped inside to inform the president of his visitor. An exasperated and slightly embarrassed clerk was shuffled out of the office in front of Mr. Taylor who quickly stepped toward Tate with his hand extended and a broad smile on his face.

"Mr. Saint! How good to see you, my, my, my, how long has it been?" and led the way into his office. Tate motioned for the ladies to follow and they did, Vinny with a surprised expression painting her face. The three were seated, and Tate began, "Mr. Taylor, this is my wife, Maggie," motioning to the redhead, "And I believe you know Mrs. Finney, who I recently found out is my aunt!"

"Your aunt?" he looked to Vinny and asked, "I had no idea."

"Nor did I, until they stopped at my Inn and I did a little inquiring. His mother was my sister, Eleanor, and they lived in Cape Girardeau."

"Oh, my, isn't that interesting," he turned to Tate, "Now, Tate, may I call you that?" and with a nod from Tate, he continued, "How may we be of service?"

"My wife and daughter will be staying in St. Louis for my daughter's education, and she will need access to our deposits as she has need."

"Of course, of course." He was writing as he listened and waited for more.

"And we will be doing some spending in the next few days. I would like some coin to take care of that, and I would like to know what our balance is now."

"Of course, of course. You will excuse me just a moment?" he said as he rose from his big chair behind the desk. He went to the door, motioned for the clerk, whispered instructions to the man, and then returned to his chair.

When the clerk returned, even before he looked at the papers, Mr. Taylor looked to Tate and said, "By the way, you have no idea how grateful I am for your deposits. A few years back there was what is often called a run on the bank, and if it hadn't been for your gold bars for our reserves, we might have gone under. As it was, one of the businesswomen in town made additional deposits, and we weathered the storm. Now we are in better shape than ever before, and as usual your money is safe with us. Now," he flipped through some pages and lifted his eyes as he looked at some figures. He turned the pages, so Tate could see and pointing to the bottom of the page, "That is your balance as of today."

Tate looked, nodded, and turned the papers back to the president. "That's fine."

"So, how much would you like to take with you today?"

"Well, I'm certain a couple thousand would be fine, if you can do that in gold coin?"

Vinny and Maggie both gasped and looked to the very somber Tate and then to Mr. Taylor, who was grinning, "We can most certainly do that for you. I'll have that for you right away. Will there be anything else?"

Tate slipped two leather pouches from his belt, lay them on the desk, "If you'll put the coin in these, it will be a sight easier to carry."

"Certainly, certainly." He rose from his seat and hurried around the desk and through the door of the office.

Vinny looked to her nephew, "Well, I must say, you are full of surprises."

"Isn't he though?" added Maggie, as she smiled coyly at her man.

"How's 'bout you ladies taking the carriage to your dress shop and Sean and I'll do a little lookin' around in that Western Emporium, an' mebbe we can get that Omnibus service to take us back to the inn," suggested Tate, winking at Sean.

"Well, that'll be fine, I imagine, since the Emporium is just around the corner from the dress shop!" declared Aunt Vinny. She smiled at Maggie and Sadie, "But if I know men, those two will probably take longer in that smelly old store than we do in the Ladies Boutique!"

Tate pulled one of the leather pouches from behind his belt, counted out ten twenty-dollar gold pieces and dropped them into Maggie's drawstring bag. Her eyes lit up, and she smiled at Tate saying, "Surely you don't expect me to need that much money?"

"Well, I ain't never bought no ladies outfits an' I have no idea what they're gonna cost. 'sides, you're buyin' for two."

She leaned over closer, "I see you brought all our rifles, you know I won't have need of one so you could give that to Sean."

"I know, but we'll see what they have, but at least I want the gunsmiths to give 'em a good goin' over. I might do some tradin', ya' just never know!" he answered, grinning.

"Ummmhummm, I do too know," responded a smiling Maggie. She knew her husband and her son, and she knew they, like most men of those times, would want the newest and the best of whatever the Emporium offered.

WHEN TATE and Sean stepped in the double doors of the Emporium, they stopped, and took a deep whiff of the interior. Leather, gun oil, trap grease, wood, gunpowder, and other smells permeated the place, and Tate smiled. After the stench of the city with sewers, horse manure, and every other disgusting odor, the smell of what some would call manhood was refreshing. He grinned at his son and opened his eyes to the dimly lit interior.

Both father and son stood mesmerized as they looked. The entire wall to their right held gun racks, floor to ceiling, with more rifles that Sean thought existed. The back wall was covered with a variety of traps, from simple rabbit snares to massive jawed bear traps, with more beaver traps than any other. Racks stood in the midst of the store heavily laden with outerwear of every sort. Wall shelves held blankets, britches, shirts, and boots. Everywhere they looked, goods of all manner were stacked high. A long glass front counter stood out from the wall of rifles and behind it stood a familiar face.

Horace Whitcomb stood watching the expressions on the faces of two so fresh from the mountains, a treat he often savored when the customer was new to the city. He knew the store was impressive to first-timers that had only seen sutler stores at frontier forts or the limited wares at trading posts. "Mr. Saint! So good to see you. How may I be of assistance?"

Tate was startled to hear his name called, but quickly responded and walked to the counter where Horace waited. He placed the two Sharps on the counter, motioned to Sean to put the two Hawkens alongside and spoke to Horace, "Well, Mr. Whitcomb," but was interrupted.

"Please, Horace would be fine."

"Then, I'm Tate and this is Sean," replied Tate, laying his hand on his son's shoulder.

"Are you interested in trading these rifles in on others?" asked a grinning Horace, anticipating a good sale.

"Well, I'd like to have your gunsmiths that you spoke so highly about, take a look at 'em and give 'em a good once over, fix anything they think needs fixin'. You know, make sure they won't fail us in the middle of a fight."

The grin faded, but Horace answered, "Of course, of course. But may I show you some of our fine firearms in the meantime? It'll take a couple days for the smiths to do the work on these," motioning to the weapons on the counter.

Tate grinned, "Sure, sure. I'm always interested in whatever might be newer an' better. Whatcha got?"

"Now, would these be for hunting or protection?"

Tate chuckled and shook his head, "Friend, where we live that's purty much the same thing. Cuz where we are just about anything you find will either stick ya', bite'cha, eat'cha, claw ya', or kill ya. An' anything that's got four legs, fins, or scales, ya' gotta fight 'em 'fore ya eat 'em. And that ain't includin' all the two-legged animals."

The young man had to laugh at Tate's description and looked at the rifles on the counter. "I see, well the newest thing that most gun builders are going for is a repeater."

"Repeater?" asked Tate.

"Yessir, these," pointing to the rifles on the counter, "as you know, are single shot rifles. After each firing, you have to reload. But a repeater holds several rounds, and you can shoot many times without reloading."

"Ya don't say. Ya' got any o' those here?"

"Yessir. Let me set these aside, and I'll show you what we have."

Within moments, Horace had gathered three rifles and lay them on the counter. He picked up the largest rifle and cradled it in both hands, "This is a Dreyse needle gun, invented by a German gunsmith, Johann Nicolaus von Dreyse. It is a breech loader similar to the Sharps and uses a paper cartridge also. Now we understand this company is working on a true repeater, but it is not yet available. So, this rifle would not be an improvement over the Sharps, but I thought you might be interested in this mechanism that is different than the Sharps. ." He worked the bolt action to show the loading of the rifle, then handed it to Tate.

Tate lifted it to his shoulder, took aim down the barrel, lowered the rifle and hefted it. "It's too heavy on the front end," he lowered the butt to the floor, looked at the muzzle, then handed the rifle back to Horace. "It's not a big enough caliber for what we need."

Horace took the rifle, leaned it against the counter and pointed to the second and third, "These are Colt rifles, similar in action to the revolvers. Each revolver had six loads, but the difference is this one is a shotgun."

Tate nodded his head, "I'm familiar with these. I've seen some, don't know too many men that like 'em. Ain't got no use for a shotgun."

"You don't hunt birds?" asked Horace, a little surprised.

"Oh, we take birds alright. But it's easier takin' 'em with our bows, quieter too. That way you can get more without scarin' the rest off."

"I see, you're an archer as well?"

Tate looked at the man, glanced at the grinning face of his son, and said, "You could say that."

"Well, let me show you something that I think will be more suited to what you need. It's brand new, and we're the only shop to have any. Matter of fact, the manufacturer sent several for our gunsmiths to try out and give their feedback on, but I might be able to get one or two for you." He walked quickly away, carrying the Colts and Needle gun to replace them. When he returned, he had two rifles that resembled the Sharps in configuration and size. But he grinned as he held one out to Tate, "This is the newest, straight from the manufacturer. This is a Spencer Repeater." After Tate took the rifle, Horace continued. "This holds one cartridge in the chamber and seven more in a tube in the buttstock. You can shoot a total of eight times before reloading. It uses this cartridge," he held out a copper cartridge for Tate to examine. "This rifle is comparable to the Sharps in power. Although it is called a .56-.56, it is actually a .52 caliber cartridge with 45 grains of powder and is accurate to five hundred yards."

Tate had lifted the rifle to his shoulder, feeling the heft of the weapon. But upon hearing the statistics from Horace, he lowered the rifle, looked at Horace, then examined the buttstock to see where the rifle held the extra rounds.

"Similar to the Sharps, you have to lower the lever to eject the spent round, but the next round is automatically inserted in the chamber as you close the lever. You do have to cock the hammer, but you don't have to use a percussion cap. Those are a part of the cartridge."

Tate looked at the man, "You don't say. Now if that don't beat all." He looked to Sean who held the second rifle at his shoulder, taking aim down the barrel with the ramp split sight and the front blade. "Whatchu think Sean?"

"It feels fine, Pa. If it does everything Horace says, it

sounds like a fine weapon."

Tate looked at the young clerk, "What about the cartridges? They costly?"

"Not much more than loading your own, that is, powder and lead, swabs, etc. and it is very convenient and speedy. Although you won't find the cartridges available right away, the manufacturer provided us with an ample supply that would hold you for some time."

"With two rifles, I'd need at least five hundred rounds each."

The clerk's eyebrows lifted, and his eyes grew large, "Five hundred rounds? Each?"

"Well, we don't get into town but once every five or six years. Course we do get to the tradin' post ever now an' again."

"I see, well, I will have to check with our smiths and Mr. Dimick, but we might be able to provide that. You know, of course, these rifles are rather expensive. Because they are in limited supply now, these would be fifty-five dollars each." He watched Tate to see his reaction to the price, but when the man didn't flinch or even look up, he continued. "And here is another item that might interest you," he lifted a revolver from the counter behind him and extended it to Tate. "This is a Colt Army Model 1860. Just out, and it is similar to the Dragoon you carry, but is lighter, faster loading, and in .44 caliber."

AFTER ALMOST TWO hours of picking out supplies, examining new products, considering all their wants and needs, Tate and Sean waited while Horace tallied up their goods. "With the two Spencers, two Colt Army revolvers, the ammunition, and the other goods, that comes to a tidy amount." When he finished, he turned to sales ticket around for Tate to see the total, watched as he nodded his head, and when Tate pulled up the pouch and began counting out twenty-dollar gold pieces, his eyes grew wide with surprise.

"Excuse me, sir! Would you happen to be Mr. Saint?" the inquiring voice came from the end of the counter, and when Tate turned to look, he saw a man of average height but with mutton-chop whiskers and a dark frock coat over lighter trousers, holding a soft crowned hat in his hand as he spoke.

"Yes, I am. And who might you be?"

"Good, good, I was hoping to find you. My name is Edward James Delacroix, and I am in need of a guide and scout for an adventure out west. Mr. John Richards said you would be the man for the job, was he right?"

"I don't know, Mr. Delacroix. Just what is this 'adventure' all about?"

"Oh, I'm sorry. We are forming a Brigade to hunt buffalo. It seems there's some wet-behind-the-ears lieutenant out west name of Philip Sheridan that has some connection to some politicians like Congressman Thomas Ritchey and John Fremont," at the mention of Fremont, Tate winced and was noticed by the speaker, but he continued, "and they want a group of their cronies to see the great herds of buffalo and the Indians that depend on them."

Tate turned back to Horace, "Are we finished here?"

"Yessir, of course if you still want your Sharps, that will take a couple of days."

Tate had traded the Hawkens in on the Spencers but wanted to keep the big buffalo guns as back-up to the new rifles. "Since you know where we're staying, can you have everything brought out to the Inn at the same time?"

"Certainly," answered the very pleased clerk.

"Good." Tate turned to Delacroix, "Now, how 'bout us goin' somewhere for some coffee and talk about this brigade?"

CHAPTER NINE
BRIGADE

THEY WERE SEATED AT A TABLE BY THE WINDOW IN THE Burgess & Co. diner on Market Street. Once they were served their coffee, Tate looked to the man called Delacroix across the table. His thin hair and receding hairline were accentuated by the thick muttonchop whiskers that obscured his ears from view, giving his overall appearance a somewhat skewed look. His brow was wrinkled, and his single bushy eyebrow hovered over the wide dark eyes like a curtain about to fall. The man wiped his nose with a kerchief and tucked the rag into his coat pocket as he leaned on the table to begin his pitch but was interrupted by the mountain man with a question.

"Did John Richards tell you why he was so upset with me that he recommended you use me as a guide?"

"Oh, no sir, I mean, he wasn't upset at all. No sir. On the contrary, because we have secured his services and his wagons, he said he wouldn't undertake this adventure without a capable guide, and he thought you were the only man competent enough!"

"So, Richards is going too? That's a horse of a different color."

Delacroix scowled, "Pardon me?"

"Never mind. Just tell me about this grand adventure and what we might be in for."

"Well, there is a group of young men, all college class-mates, and sons of important and influential people, that need to see the west in all its, well, for lack of a better term, glory. My contact, Mr. Johnathan Q. Williams, believes these young men will be the leaders of our great nation one day, and he proposed the idea they get familiar with the frontier. He suggested a buffalo hunt. He believed that would help them to understand the savage red man, and the rugged wilderness."

"The savage red man?" inquired Tate, knowing exactly what he was referring to but wanting to have a better idea of this man's understanding, or lack of it.

"You know, the wild Indians!"

Tate slowly nodded his head, "Continue."

"Well, some of these young men have connections with the men that build railroads, and it was thought they might see the 'lay of the land' so to speak. Others are connected with or have aspirations in politics and could be influential in the forming of new states, etcetera, etcetera. Frankly, I believe they're just a bunch of spoiled rich kids whose fathers want to get them off their hands for a while."

"Well, if all they want to do is shoot some buffalo, we can take a week or two, go to Kansas territory, shoot some and come back."

"Oh, mercy me, no! It's more than just shooting buffalo. They need to see the west! Mr. Richards is the trader at Fort Bernard, and he suggested it would be good for them to even go so far as the Rocky Mountains!"

"Oh, he did, did he?"

"So, here's what I was thinking," he leaned forward on his elbows, appearing conspiratorially, "Mr. Richards . . . "

"Are you going with us?"

"Oh, heavens no!"

"Then how 'bout you let me, and Mr. Richards do the planning? You get with him, let him know how many there will be and how many wagons will be needed, and anything else you think pertinent. Then, if I decide to go, I'll get with John, and we'll iron things out."

"Oh, I suppose that would be alright. But Mr. Richards said he would like to get underway by the end of the week. Will that be satisfactory?"

"If I decide to go, that will be fine."

"Oh, and we haven't discussed your compensation." He drew a folded paper from his inside breast pocket, unfolded it and smoothed out the wrinkles. He turned it to face Tate, "You can read, can't you?"

Tate's eyebrows lowered in a frown, he nodded and pulled the paper close. He looked at the number, thought about the time and work involved, then lifted his eyes to Delacroix. "Just what is your connection with this bunch of snobs?"

"Hummph, I am the attorney selected to represent them," he declared, somewhat pompously.

"I see. Then add another $100 to that figure and the promise to pay another $100 upon the return of the survivors, and I'll give it my utmost consideration."

Delacroix' eyes widened, and he looked askance to Tate, "Survivors?"

"We will be going into dangerous country, crossing the homelands of, oh, about a half-dozen different tribes of the 'savage red man' that aren't too happy with the current politicians, and that's not even mentioning the grizzly bears, buffalo stampedes, mountain lions, and other obstacles. It is nothing short of life-threatening anytime we go into what you call the rugged wilderness. Would you do all that for that much money?" he pointed to the figure at the bottom of the page.

"Heavens no! You couldn't pay me enough!" He looked at Tate, down at the figures, and added, "I'm certain your terms will be satisfactory."

"And all that money is to be paid to Maggie Saint, my wife, now residing at Finney's Inn just south of town with my aunt, LaVinia."

Tate turned to his son, put his hand on his shoulder, and said, "We need to get back to the womenfolk, ya' reckon?"

"Sure, Pa."

The men stood, shook hands with the attorney and excused themselves. When they stepped from the doorway, Sean anxiously asked, "Are we gonna do it, Pa? Go with them fellas, I mean?"

"Son, we'll have to talk to your ma 'fore we decide anything. Now, how 'bout us catchin' a ride on that omnibus comin'?"

"SAY, we need to go south on Carondelet to Finney's Inn. Will this thing get us there?" hollered Tate to the driver of the omnibus. The odd-looking vehicle had stopped at the corner, and the driver held a taut rein on the matched pair of dapple-grey draft horses. He looked down at the two buckskin-clad men, nodded his derby topped head and said, "The Finney Inn is the last stop for the day. Climb aboard, an' you'll have a better view from up top here!" The driver motioned to the seats directly behind him.

Tate motioned Sean to go to the back, and they climbed the stairs at the rear of the omnibus and took their seats directly behind the driver. The other seats were unoccupied, with the other riders choosing the seats inside on the lower level. The omnibus had larger wheels at the rear, and the driver's seat was just forward of the top seats, his feet on a bar level with the rumps of the powerful draft horses. The big shod hooves of the two horses clattered on the cobblestones as the big wagon-like vehicle negotiated the corner. The driver leaned back, "So, where you fellas from?"

"We live in the mountains, the Rocky Mountains out west. Came in for some supplies an' such," answered Tate.

"First time in the big city?"

"No, been here a'fore, didn't like it then either."

The hefty driver chuckled, "Can't blame ya' for that, no sir. Gettin' too big fer me, too."

While Tate and the driver talked, Sean was busy taking in the sights. Awed by the towering buildings and the many people, he swiveled his head back and forth, not wanting to miss anything. He was so involved in looking, he didn't notice when the bus stopped, and others boarded until he heard a giggle from the other side. He looked to see two girls, both about his age, talking with their hands to their mouths as they giggled and looked at him. He felt the heat rise in his neck, and he knew he was blushing, but he had never seen any girls his age that weren't Indians. He dropped his eyes to his hands until one of the girls spoke.

Sean didn't hear what the girl said, but when he looked at her, he knew she had spoken to him. "Pardon me? I didn't hear what you said."

The two girls looked like they could be sisters, both attired in similar dresses, dark colored and long with light colored ribbons in a row near the hemline. Cream colored lace decorated the bodices and stood around their necks. Both girls had shawls over their shoulders and drawstring bags on their wrists. One had long blonde curls and the other had auburn hair that caught the sun and seemed to glow as

Sean looked. The auburn-haired girl asked, "Why are you dressed like that? Don't you have real clothes?"

Sean couldn't tell if she was actually curious or just mocking him, but he chose to answer, "These are buckskins and where we are from, this is the best thing to wear. Your 'city clothes' wouldn't last long in the wilderness."

The girl blushed and lowered her eyes, looking at her hands on her lap. She glanced back to Sean, "I'm sorry, I've never seen anyone in, what'd you call them, buckskins?"

"Yes, they're buckskins. Made from the leather of deer or elk. These were made by my mother and her friend, White Fawn of the Arapaho." Sean was proud of his buckskins with the beadwork and fringe, they fit him well and were soft and comfortable, unlike what he imagined the stiff and scratchy britches and shirts he saw others wearing.

"Then where are you from that you wear buckskins?" the words seemed to be spit from the lips of the blonde.

"We live out west in the Rocky Mountains," replied Sean, proudly, determined to not allow the city girls to make light of him.

The auburn girl scowled at her friend and turned back to Sean, "That seems so far away. Have you ever been to the city before?"

"No, I haven't. This is my first time. And yes, the mountains are a long way from here. We left in early spring and pulled in yesterday."

"Oh my, that's what, three months?"

"Ummhumm."

The omnibus pulled to a halt and the driver called, "Park!"

The girls looked to one another and stood to leave, the auburn-haired one turned to Sean, "It was nice visiting with you. I hope you have a nice stay."

Sean stood, "Thank you, it was nice talking with you too."

He watched as the girls started down the stairs, the

friendlier of the two turned to wave at Sean and he blushed again as he raised his hand to wave back. He sat back down and looked to his pa grinning at him, "Made a friend, didja?"

"Ah, I dunno. Prob'ly never see 'em again anyway. But they sure were purty!"

Both men and the driver had a good laugh and the driver cracked his whip over the heads of the horses causing them to lean into their traces and start the omnibus moving again. It was less than a quarter hour later when they stopped at the end of the driveway with the sign, *Finney's Inn*. Tate and Sean bid their goodbyes to the driver as they stepped from the omnibus and started up the roadway.

CHAPTER TEN
PREPARATION

"The way I got it figgered, we won't be needin' any more wagons than what we came out with. The sightseers are s'posed to be bringin' their own gear an' such, an' they'll use the wagons. Course, I'll prob'ly have to teach 'em how to handle a team, but ain't no use in takin' on extra help to drive the wagons when they can do it themselves. You can put your outfit in one o' the wagons too. An' I'm loadin' a couple the freighters a little light in case we get some buffler hides on the way out. Now, once we get to the fort, I'll be sendin' at least four freighters with 'em to haul hides an' the roustabouts an' teamsters will see to the skinnin' an' loadin'." Richards looked to Tate as he paused. They were sitting atop the rail fence behind the barn of the farm where Richards spent his off time. The field beyond the corral held a sizable herd of mules and horses, all knee deep in green grass.

With each freighter needing four mules and heavier loads requiring a six-up, and the covered wagons with two or four mules, depending on the load, the trip west would require a herd of at least sixty mules and twelve to fifteen horses. Tate looked to the field, "You got a wrangler for the animals?"

"Yeah, old man Biddle and his son been handlin' mules an' horses for as long as I've known 'em. Since his wife died last year he's been wantin' to go west so I figger both of 'em will be good hands."

"Cooky stayin' with the wagons?" asked Tate, referring to the cook that came east with them.

"Ummmhummm. An' he likes to ride up top with the teamsters. I had to make special room in one o' the freighters for all his cookin' paraphernalia and the foodstuffs. But we're still countin' on you bringin' in some game every now an' then."

"So, just how many of these college kids are you gonna hafta babysit?" asked Tate, grinning.

"I ain't babysittin' anybody! I'm gonna set 'em all straight on that 'fore we leave! But there's eight of 'em an' they got some helpers or servants or somethin' comin' along too. I think there's four of 'em.. Some of 'em have their own horses but even if they don't, they'll ride in the wagons and take care of their own cookin' and such. This is supposed to be a 'grand adventure' for all of 'em." Both men chuckled at the thought of a 'grand adventure,' all the while knowing this trip would be the making or breaking of these young men, and quite possibly the death of some.

John asked, "So, how'd the missus take it when you told her you were goin' back west?"

Tate dropped his head, lifted it, "I didn't *tell* her, we talked it over. She said she knew all along that I wouldn't be staying here in the city. I think her words were, 'The city would be the death of you, Tate. I know you belong in the mountains and you know I would be there with you, but our daughter . . . ' It's gonna be tough without her and Sadie, but both Sean and I belong in the mountains. His education won't be lacking anything, we've got two boxes of books we're takin' with us, and I'm certain we'll both learn a lot. But Sadie girl, that's different. She's got a sharp mind and is anxious to learn all she can, and she will too." He dropped his head again and sighed heavily.

Richards put his hand on Tate's shoulder, saying nothing, but meaning everything. That's the way it is between men that are good friends and have been through the fire, a hand on the shoulder says more than words could express.

Tate lifted his eyes to the animals in the field, looked back to John and added, "Since you'll be comin' right by the Inn, I figgered it'd be just as easy for me to load up our stuff there and take off from there, if that's alright with you?"

"Sure, sure. I'm just glad you're comin' with us. I think those college kids can learn a lot from us old codgers!"

"Old!?! I ain't old! You watch your language there! I ain't been so insulted in a long time!" Tate grinned and slid from the rail to drop to the ground. Sean had stayed at the Inn and now Tate's only companion was Lobo, the big grey wolf that felt out of sorts with all the noises and such of the city. Tate slipped the tie on Shady's reins, swung aboard the mousy colored grulla and with a simple wave motioned Lobo along-side, and they started back to the Inn.

CONVERSATION at the dinner table was monopolized by Horace Whitcomb, mostly with questions about the trip that Tate and Sean would soon be embarking upon. The brothers had never been outside of St. Louis except for short buggy rides in the country and to think of traveling for months into the wilderness was exciting to them. Horace especially wanted to know about the Indians and the animals, needing to broaden his knowledge for the benefit of his position at the emporium.

"So, tell me, Mr. Saint, have you ever shot one of those grizzly bears?"

Tate, not feeling too talkative replied, "Yes. On occasion."

"Now, I've read about the bears, but are the grizzly as big as they say?" quizzed the young man, skeptically.

Tate looked at the man, glanced around, and seeing the ten-foot ceiling overhead, he pointed, "Well, I've seen them mark their territory with claw marks on the trees, higher than the walls there. That's better'n ten feet. And I've seen 'em stand on their hind legs an' paw at the air as they growled a warning, and the top o' their head was easily at the nine-foot mark."

Horace and his brother looked at the wall, mouths ajar, and back at Tate to see if he was joshing them. But his serious expression told them otherwise.

Tate continued, "An' my wife there, shot one in our front yard that measured almost eight-foot square. That's eight foot from the tip of his tail to the tip of his nose and eight foot from the claws on one foot to the claws on the other. An' their claws are longer'n your fingers."

The young men both looked to a smiling Maggie and back to Tate. Horace pointed to her, "She did? What with?"

Maggie answered, "My Sharps," matter-of-factly, without pausing as she reached for her cup of tea.

The brothers stared at her, expecting more, but she continued with her meal quietly. Horace was especially surprised because he had heard that it took a man to stand behind the big buffalo gun and she wasn't any bigger than a whisper.

Maggie was enjoying the attention and was laughing inside at the men at the table that thought a woman was not capable of doing what only a man was supposed to do, especially handling firearms.

"Course, both my youngsters are quite handy with rifles as well. Both of 'em have taken an elk and more. But, when they had a chance to kill a bear, they just made a pet out of him instead," said Tate, proudly.

Both youngsters beamed at their father's praise and Sadie piped in, "And we named him Buster! He was a cinnamon bear!"

Henry Whitcomb looked at the girl and asked, "Cinnamon?"

"Ummhumm, that's because his fur was the color of cinnamon, you know, reddish. Pa says he was actually a black bear, but when they have a coat like that, they're called cinnamon," stated the girl, pretentiously.

"You actually had a pet bear?"

"Of course, and he was friends with Lobo, our pet wolf," added Sadie.

The brothers looked to Tate to judge the veracity of the little girl's remarks, but he nodded his head in agreement. Horace said, "It's is almost unbelievable that you had these wild animals for pets, especially for your children."

"Oh, our wolves are with us. They're out in the barn!" informed Sadie.

Again, the brothers looked to Tate, Horace asking, "Wolves? More than one?"

Tate explained, "Well, I started with Lobo, but one day, not too long ago, he brought another one home. We think Indy is a pup from one of his night-time romances. But, yes, they both are out in the barn. We couldn't just leave them behind, now could we?"

"I suppose not, but I just can't imagine wolves in St. Louis!" declared Henry.

"Well, we're not actually *in* St. Louis," interjected LaVinia, reminding the many guests that they were indeed out of the city limits and in what was considered the 'country.'

The conversation continued until Mary McCarthy, Aunt Vinny's helper, brought out two deep berry pies that elicited oohs and ahhhs from everyone at the table. LaVinia did the cutting and Mary passed the dessert plates to the guests. By the time everyone had received their plates, Sean was leaning back in the chair, smiling at his empty plate. "Aunt Vinny, that was the best!"

"Well thank you Sean, but Mary actually made these, and she is quite good at it, don't you think?"

"Yes ma'am. We don't get to have fresh berry pie this early in the mountains, but Ma makes a good one whenever we can get some."

"Well, these pies have a combination of blueberries, lingonberries, and raspberries. She also makes a wonderful strawberry pie."

Sean grinned at Mary, "Me an Pa ain't leavin' till sometime tomorrow . . . " he suggested, hoping for a strawberry pie.

Maggie corrected, "It's Pa and I aren't leaving . . ."

Sean hung his head at the correction, mumbling, "Pa and I aren't . . . "

Mary smiled and answered, "Aye, an' it just might be that ye'll be graced with a strawberry pie, if ye behave yourself."

Tate and Maggie chuckled, and Maggie said, "Bribery with anything sweet will always get the best out of that boy."

WHEN THE GOODS were delivered from the Western Emporium, Horace had come along to direct the driver to the Inn and to help with the unloading. At the direction of Tate, the bundles, satchels, and bags were stacked on the veranda, but he took the rifles and pistols inside to show Maggie. After he explained each of the weapons and set them aside, she asked, "I notice you kept both Sharps, won't the new rifles, the Spencers, do just as well?"

"Well, probably, but I ain't in any hurry to get rid of the

Sharps. They have served us well and I just, well, I'm just not confident in the new rifles just yet. Since these are some o' the first, there's probably gonna be a few things that don't work just right or something, and I don't wanna be caught without a good rifle. You know how it is." He looked up at his redhead, grinning.

Maggie dropped her head and softly replied, "Yes, I know how it is," then looking back to Tate, "and you know that is why Sadie and I are here."

THE EARLY PART of the next day, Tate and Maggie walked around the property, hand in hand, sharing the few moments before parting. "Would it be better if I send the letters to Fort Bernard or Laramie?" asked Maggie.

"Oh, prob'ly Bernard. I'm sure Richards will do his best to get 'em to me or at least let me know somehow. What with the army takin' over Laramie, ya' just never know what them soldier boys will do with anything."

"By the way, about that gold the banker spoke of . . . " asked Maggie, looking up at Tate with a bit of a smile.

"Oh that. I told you we had some money in the bank," answered Tate, somewhat elusive.

"Is that all you're going to say?" She was still smiling coyly as she looked sideways while they walked.

"Well, it was old Spanish gold. Legend has it that in the San Luis Valley near our cabin, back, oh, 'bout a hundred and fifty years or so, some conquistadores captured a band of Indians with gold ornaments. They forced them to show where they found the gold, made slaves out of the Indians and had them do the digging. The Spanish smelted it into bars, stashed it in a part of the mine waiting until they had it all, and planned on taking it out. But the Indians had other ideas. They rose up against them, killed 'em all and the priests at the mission as well. And I just happened to find the stash and brought some of it out and put it in the bank."

"Oh, that's all, huh? And where was this mine where you found the gold."

Tate grinned, chuckled, and said, "What? You don't know? Why Maggie, you've been in it many times?"

Maggie stopped where they stood, pulled at Tate's arm to turn him toward her, and asked, "What do you mean? I've never been in a mine before?"

"Well, we didn't call it a mine, we called it a storage cave. Remember?"

"You mean the cavern behind the cabin in the Sangre de Cristo's?"

"Ummmhumm, that's the place."

They laughed together until it dawned on Maggie what Tate had said about the gold. "Wait, you said you brought *some* of it out. You mean there's more?"

"Yup, but it was too heavy to carry an' 'sides, didn't need any more."

Again, they laughed as they came to a bench made from a big log and sat down. It was a special time, yet neither wanted the moments to end. The future was uncertain at best, and fearful at most. Since they first met at Bent's fort so many years ago, their times apart had been limited by circumstance. But there was always the anticipated reunion. But this time was so different, and both knew the likelihood of never being together again was a real possibility. They were living in uncertain times, Indian uprisings in the west, and with the political climate regarding slavery, even the civilized portions of the country were perilous.

Maggie held tightly to Tate's hand and with her other hand on his arm, they walked close beside one another, deep in thought and dreading the coming separation. But love requires sacrifice and family love demands commitment and a willingness to make that sacrifice.. "I will pray for you every day! And I know you will take care of our son, but I have to say it anyway, please watch over him!"

Tate put his arm around her shoulder and drew her near, "And you watch over our daughter and yourself." They joined hands and shared a special time of prayer for one another, their children, and the uncertain days ahead. They embraced and clung to one another tightly until they heard the call of Sean from the veranda. The wagons were coming.

TATE AND SEAN HUNG BACK A WAYS FROM THE LAST WAGON, wanting one last look and wave to the girls. Once the road bent beyond the trees and the Inn was out of sight, Tate turned to Sean, "These first few days, you and I won't have much to do 'cept maybe bring in some meat ever now and then. I'm thinkin' we're gonna have our work cut out for us what with these city boys not knowin' much about the wilderness. So, we're prob'ly gonna have to keep an eye on the trail before us as much as the goin's on behind us. Know what I mean?"

"Sure Pa, but just what is it we need to be watchin' for?"

"Well, from what I understand, these men are all from influential families and none of them have been out of the city. They're supposed to have their own rifles and such, but I don't know if any of 'em know much about hunting or surviving in the wild. . So, just keep an eye on 'em, keep 'em outta trouble if you can, and watch and learn. We might find we have to give them a little wilderness education to go along with all their book learnin'."

Sean grinned, nodded his head, and chuckled. "I'm thinkin' this is gonna be educational for all of us."

Lobo trotted alongside Tate's grulla Shady, and Indy, the black wolf that was claimed by Sadie, trotted beside Sean's Appaloosa, Dusty. One appearing as the shadow image of the other. Little had to be said between the two as the conversation between like-minded kindred spirits was more of anticipation and understanding that was the fruit of years together. As the two made their camp apart from the rest of the wagons, theirs was one of vigilance and guardianship. Although the country they were passing through in the past two weeks showed little danger, their habits were set for they knew the coming days would present unknown and often life-threatening challenges for everyone in their charge.

ON THE EVE of the fourteenth day out of St. Louis, the train camped on the flats near the small community of Harrisonville. Although the town was small, the local smithy was a friend of Richards' and skilled at anything and everything about wagon and harness repair. John Richards told Tate, "We'll take a couple days rest here. Got a couple things needin' repair 'fore we move on. It's the usual, you know, the 'shakedown' of the gear when we get on the trail. If'n there's anything you need in town, the general store ain't too big, but he keeps it purty well stocked."

Both Tate and Sean were seated at the cookfire for the freighters, Lobo and Indy lying beside them, and Tate looked to Richards, "So, what'chu think o' these city kids?"

John slowly shook his head, "One thing for sure, I'm glad you're the one what's gonna be doin' most o' the tendin' to 'em."

"And just what do you mean by that?"

"Wal, have you noticed those 'helpers' they have with 'em,

I'm thinkin' all four o' those men are slaves! I mean, the way a couple them fellas order 'em around and such, it's like those 'helpers' don't have any say in it."

Tate knew Missouri was a slave state but that many had been given their freedom through manumission, while the territories still did not allow slavery, yet with the ongoing struggle in Kansas, that might change.

"That Delacroix fella didn't say anything about takin' slaves along on this 'grand adventure!'" spat Tate, showing his disgust.

"An' that ain't all, what with the fracas in Kansas territory, what happens when we run up against some o' them Redlegs or Slavers?"

"Have you figgered out which one o' them is the leader o' this bunch?"

"I dunno if they've chosen themselves a leader as such, but the one that seems to do all the talkin' for 'em is that big 'un, Patrick Hutton, an' the other'n is the one they call Justis."

Tate shook his head and picked up a stick to poke at the coals of the fire, "Mebbe you need to be talkin' to them an' find out 'bout them 'helpers.' Cuz, you're their keeper, not me, at least until we get to the fort."

"You would have to throw that up to me, wouldn'tchu?"

Tate grinned, "Yup, an' if I have to, I'll remind you of it just 'bout everday!"

"So, FELLAS, HOW'S IT GOIN' so far? You've had a couple weeks on the trail and have a taste of the life we're headin' into, so, what'chu think?"

Tate was standing at the edge of the circle of light from the cookfire used by the servants of the college men. Most of the group were seated around the fire and looked to Tate as he questioned them. This was his first time speaking to the group and they were rather surprised at his question. Several of them looked at one another and finally the one called Patrick spoke up. "I have to say that we're a little disappointed. All we've seen is a long, dirty trail and nothing exciting at all." Tate would learn later that Patrick was the self-appointed leader of the group, his assumption coming from his years as a prominent figure on the campus of Yale. He was a nephew of the Industrialist, Andrew Carnegie, and was quick to use his uncle's influence to further his own agenda. He was about the same size as Tate, standing just over six feet with broad shoulders, dark eyes resting on high cheekbones, with wavy dark hair that hid the tops of his ears. He showed confidence and even arrogance, a trait that Tate would find common among these men that used their connections without reservation.

"Hear, hear," answered some of the others, lifting glasses of wine toward one another.

"Just what kind of excitement were you expecting?"

"Isn't this supposed to be a hunting expedition?" asked the man that sat beside the leader. He was called Justis Williams, a brother-in-law of sorts, to the Vanderbilts. His sister had married into the Vanderbilt family and they had graciously accepted her entire Williams family into their social circle. Justis was just under six feet, short-cropped light brown hair, plain-featured face and shoulders that were slightly stooped, but his physical features spoke of strength. He had been a long-time companion of the leader, Patrick.

"Have any of you done any huntin'?"

Malcolm Whitehurst and Erastus Throckmorton both lifted their hands, grinning at one another and looking to Tate. "We have."

Patrick and Clifton Burge both added, "We have also."

Tate nodded toward the two seated together that answered first, "And what have you two fellas hunted?"

They looked at one another and back to Tate with an expression of disdain, "Fox, of course, what else?"

He looked to Patrick with raised eyebrows to await their answer, "Bird hunting by the lake at our summer home," stated Patrick.

Tate then turned to Burge who answered, "Same."

"And the rest of you fellas?" inquired Tate, looking from one to the other, as each man shook his head.

"Do all of you have rifles?" asked Tate, knowing they had been told to bring the proper arms.

Patrick spoke for them, "Yes, we all have rifles for hunting," his answer one of contempt toward the man that questioned their ability to properly prepare for the trip.

Tate randomly looked to one man, "You, what type of rifle did you bring?"

Louis Reale, a nephew of an executive with the Pennsylvania Railroad, answered, "I have a Dreyse needle gun, .61 caliber."

Tate nodded his head, remembering the needle gun at Dimick's Western Emporium. "Have you shot it very much?"

"A few times."

Tate looked to another, "And you?"

David Smits, the only Medical College graduate, answered, "I have a Springfield, Model 1855, .58 caliber."

"Practice with it?" asked Tate.

"A little."

As Tate went around the circle, a variety of answers were given. One had a Merrill carbine, two had Colt Revolving carbines, two had Sharps, and one had a Hawken. None had practiced very much with their rifles, thinking they were competent enough after firing their weapons a few times at stationary targets.

"So, you'd like to do a little hunting huh? Tell ya what I'll do, let me see, there's eight of you, so each day I'll take one of you and Sean, he's the other scout, he'll take one, and we'll give each of you an opportunity to do a little huntin' with us. Now, we ain't gonna run into any grizzlies or buffler in these next few days, but we might come acrost some Jayhawkers or some Bushwhackers. Course, they ain't like grizzlies, cuz they shoot back, but it might be excitin' 'nuff for ya. So, you choose who's goin' tomorrow, cuz we pull out 'fore the rest o' the camp an' we'll be by just 'fore daylight. Have your horses saddled an' yore gear ready when we come by or we'll just leave you behind."

He was intentionally using the mountain man vernacular to see the response he would get from the college men. But they seemed to pay little mind to his language, but close attention to his subject matter. The expressions of surprise told Tate the men knew little of Bloody Kansas and he turned his back to them before they could ask any questions. He chuckled to himself at their expressions and knew the next few days might indeed be exciting as they traveled through Kansas territory, which was still rife with conflict over the issue of slavery.

Tate stopped by the wagon used by the men for their kitchen and spoke with the 'helpers' that were busy with the clean-up after the evening meal. Tate extended his hand to the nearest man, "Evenin' gents. I'm Tate, I'm the scout and guide for this outfit."

The oldest of the group looked to Tate with wide eyes, surprised at his extended hand, and with a slow smile he reached forward to shake it, "Evenin' suh. I be Jeremiah." He turned toward the others who were already drying their hands on a dishtowel, "And this is Horatio, Johnathan, and Timothy. We're pleased to meet you suh!" Each man willingly shook Tate's hand as they were introduced. Jeremiah had dark eyes that showed a sparkle of wisdom and mischief as he smiled at Tate. The man had just a touch of grey at his temples, wrinkles across his forehead, but a smooth intelligent face. Horatio and Johnathan looked like brothers, similar size and features, but Timothy was obviously the youngest of the group and held back a ways from the others.

"So, tell me 'bout yourselves, are you all from Missouri?" asked Tate.

"Yessuh, we're from the Reale home. Massuh Louis Reale brought us along to tend to the needs of these gentlemen," answered Jeremiah.

"So, are you employed by Mr. Reale?"

"Nossuh, we all be owned by the family."

It was what Tate expected but was not happy with the hearing of it. He dropped his head before speaking again, "I see. Well fellas, for about the next week or ten days, I suggest you all stay inside the wagons during the day. You see, we'll be traveling through Kansas territory and there's been quite a bit of fighting about this issue of slavery. There are those that are called Jayhawkers or Redlegs that want to make the territory a free state. And there are others, Bushwhackers or Ruffians, that want it to be a slave state. And if any of 'em saw you fellas riding the wagons, that might be just enough to cause a big fight, even though we're not a part of the territory. So, for your own safety, I'd stay out of sight. Understand?"

"Yessuh, thank you suh. We will certainly be doin' that suh."

"Alright then. I'll let you know when we're outta the territory," answered Tate as he turned away thinking *Might even let you know when and where you can go to be free too!*

CHAPTER TWELVE
LESSONS

WHEN TATE AND SEAN RODE UP TO THE CAMP OF THE COLLEGE gang, the young men were surprised and a little concerned when they saw the big wolves beside the scouts. But when the hand signals from Tate and Sean prompted Lobo and Indy to drop to their bellies beside the horses, the men at the fire relaxed a little. The servants kept their distance on the other side of the fire from the wolves while Patrick Hutton and Justis Williams led their horses to the circle.

"Ready boys?" asked Tate as he leaned forward on the pommel.

"Is there anything we need besides our rifles?" asked Justis, looking expectantly to Tate and ignoring the scowl from Patrick.

"You might bring a blanket or two just in case we have to camp out yonder."

"Camp?! Surely you don't expect us to camp out there away from the wagons and our beds?" spat an indignant Patrick as he stepped away from his horse.

"I don't expect anything, but it's always best to be prepared for everything."

Patrick mumbled as he made his way to the wagon to retrieve a pair of blankets for him and his usual companion.

Justis looked to Tate, "Will we all be riding together?"

"Oh, mebbe, mebbe not. Depends . . . "

"Depends? On what?"

"On what we see, where we go, the usual," replied Tate, noncommittally, but enjoying the suspense he saw in the eyes of the city boy.

"Oh."

The two had not finished tying the blankets behind the cantles of the saddles when Tate reined around, followed by Sean and the wolves, and started to leave. The two friends had always been used to others following them and were surprised to find themselves hurrying to catch up to the guides.

When Tate sensed their nearness, he motioned to Patrick to ride beside him, leaving Justis to ride along with Sean. Tate glanced at Patrick, who was obviously a little uncomfortable in the stock saddle. Tate knew in the east the English style flat saddle had become popular especially with those that did fox hunting.

"So, Patrick, tell me about yourself."

"Humph, just what would you like to know?" replied the indignant and uncomfortable leader of the group.

"Well, in the west, it is not an acceptable practice to ask about nor question a man regarding his past, so you tell me anything you want me to know."

And so, it began. A young man that was quite proud of his heritage and his accomplishments was given an opportunity to brag about himself, and to try to impress this uncouth buckskinner from the mountains. So, he rattled on about his Uncle Andrew Carnegie, his prowess as captain of the rowing team, his many women friends, and his popularity among his classmates.

"So, you see, my uncle thought this grand adventure would be a good experience to see the west and what possibilities there might be for investments. He also thought some familiarity with the savages would help in evaluating the impact they might have on any future endeavors."

"And what do you think about this grand adventure?"

"Well, I, uh, I, suppose it will be a good thing."

"You mentioned investments, what do you consider the value of a human life?"

"I don't understand, what do you mean?"

"It's simple enough, what is the value of a human life?"

"Well, I suppose that would be relative to which human life."

"So, you think one life is worth more than another?"

"Certainly!"

"Your life is worth more or less than mine?" asked Tate of the young man who was growing uncomfortable with the questioning.

"Sir, I am a part of the Carnegie family and you are but a mountain man, how could you possibly compare the two?"

Tate reined up and with an elbow on the pommel of his saddle he looked at the flustered Patrick. "Now, maybe back east where your uncle can buy and sell people, you might think your life is more valuable, but out here, where you don't know which end is up and you could run into all sorts of danger, I think you will find that the life of the man that can save your life becomes mighty valuable. For instance, point out to me which direction you would go to get back to the wagons."

Patrick turned around in his saddle and pointed to their back trail, "Why, that way, of course!"

"See what I mean. While you were so busy bragging about your life, we traveled in a big circle, which you didn't notice. We are actually behind the wagons now and they are just past that cluster of trees yonder. If you had been left on your own, you would have wandered around in these woods for days before you found your way out, if then."

Tate sat upright, clucked Shady forward and motioned for Patrick to come alongside. "That's the way we're going. You never know which man is more important at any given time. There are men with extensive educations that would put your college degree to shame, and others that can't even read or write, but there might come a time that uneducated man might be more valuable to you than the one who has read or taught Plato, Socrates, Blackstone, and others. And that person that might save your life becomes all mighty important and yes, valuable, to you, even if he is a former slave, a 'savage' on the plains, or a simple man in buckskins that forgot more than you'll ever know. And when you speak of investments, any investment out west will have to be paid with the lives of many men. That might change the value of your investment considerably, especially if one of those lives is yours."

Tate looked over at the man beside him, "You see, Patrick, out here your college degree doesn't mean a thing. But what you do, how you treat others, will prove what kind of man you truly are, and you'll do well to remember that."

SEAN AND JUSTIS had been riding behind Tate and Patrick, but close enough to hear the conversation. Justis spoke quietly as he asked, "Is he always that 'preachy'?"

Sean looked at his companion, "Pa is always teaching, if that's what you mean."

"Pa? He's your father?"

"Ummhumm."

Tate led them to a sunny clearing away from the roadway. They had taken a narrow trail through the woods that topped a low knoll and dropped into the wide valley that showed an abundance of wildflowers of every conceivable color. Their clearing overlooked the roadway and Tate said, "We passed the wagons when we topped that little knoll, they'll be along in a spell and we'll have our noonin'. Sean, how 'bout you an' Justis gather up some firewood and we'll put some coffee on while Patrick here tends to the horses."

"What do you mean, 'tend'?"

"Haven't done that before, have you?" asked Tate with a wide grin. He knew the group had relied on the four servants to take care of just about everything and the college boys had done very little around their camp. "First off, take off all their gear, let 'em roll in the grass, an' then tether 'em with a long 'nuff lead so they can graze but not run off."

Tate busied himself with the coffee pot and rolling a few stones to make a fire ring. Sean had dropped an armload of dry wood and turned to get another, when Justis dropped several branches of green leafy wood beside the dry. Sean looked at the branches, up at Justis, and said, "The wood needs to be dead and dry. That way it'll burn without a lot of smoke and make a better fire."

"What difference does it make if there's smoke?"

"Around here, not much. But when you're in unfriendly country, you don't want to show where you're camped by sending up a pillar of smoke. So, it's best to get in the habit now."

Justis turned, mumbling, "You're as bad as your old man!"

Sean looked at Tate who was grinning, "Like you said, son. An educational time for us all!"

BY THE TIME their coffee was ready, the wagons had pulled up and the animals were given a chance for a drink at the small stream. Fires flared for their noon meal and all the men were ready for the food and brief rest. A rest that was over all too soon for most, but the wagons were back on the road and the scouts rode well ahead of the train.

Tate sent Sean and Justis to the far side of a stream that paralleled the roadway and he and Patrick moved off the road to ride nearer the brush at the stream's edge. Tate spoke just above a whisper, "We'll move careful like along here, mebbe jump a deer or two. Have your rifle ready."

Patrick slipped his Sharps from the scabbard under his right leg and lay it across his pommel. He eared back the hammer to place a cap on the nipple and lowered the hammer to half-cock. Lobo led the duo and suddenly froze, one forepaw lifted, and Tate knew the wolf had spotted something. Tate held up his hand to Patrick and motioned for them to dismount.

Using hand gestures, Tate told Patrick to take a position to be ready to shoot and Patrick's knee had no sooner touched the grass, when a button buck sprang from the brush to flee. Patrick brought the rifle to his shoulder, followed the buck with his muzzle and jerked the trigger to hear nothing. He had failed to bring the rifle to a full cock. He looked to the hammer, saw his error, cocked the rifle and looked for the deer, and saw nothing but a white flag of a tail disappear into the trees.

In his disappointment, the young man stood, kicked at the grass at his feet, looked to Tate, "That should have been an easy shot!" He kicked again, grumbling, "Dumb! Plain dumb!"

Tate chuckled and said, "There'll be others. If that's the worst mistake you make, you'll be alright. Just be glad it wasn't a charging Indian with his sights on your hair!"

"My hair?"

"Sure. Ain't a warrior out there that wouldn't like to have that curly hair hanging from his lance or in his lodge."

Patrick ran his fingers through his hair, thinking about what Tate had said, "They really do that?"

"Ummhumm. It's like a trophy, show's how great they were in battle. The more scalps, the more honor. Goes a long way to show the women of the village what a great man he is, and they show favor to those with lots of scalps. Hard to get a wife without a few scalps."

Tate chuckled and said, "C'mon, we got a ways to go yet."

Tate and Patrick had just mounted when a big boom from the other side of the stream startled them, but Tate just grinned, knowing Sean or his charge had fired the shot.

SEAN SAID, "You got him! Good shot!"

Justis was grinning ear to ear with the praise and the result of his shooting. But suddenly the deer, a fork-horned, in the velvet, buck, was struggling to his feet. Sean lifted his Hawken and fired. His bullet found its mark and the buck dropped again, unmoving. The two walked to the downed animal and Sean poked it with the muzzle of his rifle. It was dead. Sean looked to Justis, who was staring at the unmoving buck with a somber expression on his face. Sean asked, "First time?"

"I've never killed anything before," he said quietly.

"Well, I remember my first time, I understand. But what helped me was to get the animal dressed out and begin to see it as meat instead of a deer. Your stomach kind of takes over for your brain and mind, then it's not so bad. You'll get used to it."

Sean reloaded his rifle, motioned for Justis to do the same, and setting them aside, he started the process of dressing out the carcass. They had no sooner started when they heard the approach of Tate and Patrick as their horses came across the creek.

Patrick saw the downed deer, looked to his friend, "Did you get it?" he asked excitedly.

Before Justis could say anything, Sean said, "He sure did. Great shot, too!"

Justis looked to Sean, grinned, and nodded his head in thanks. Tate began explaining to the two about the proper way of dressing out a kill and had the two take over the work from Sean. In just a short while the carcass was finished. The head, legs and entrails in a pile nearby to provide fodder for the carrion and coyotes, with Indy and Lobo satisfied with their share of the innards. The carcass had been cut in quarters and each man strapped a quarter on behind their cantles and were ready to return to the road. Tate motioned to the approaching wagons and said, "That deer'll take care of supper, maybe a little left for breakfast, but we'll need more tomorrow!"

THE SECOND DAY OUT OF HARRISONVILLE, THE WAGONS WERE well into Kansas Territory and Tate and Sean had two new understudies riding with them. Louis Reale, the nephew of the divisional director of the Pennsylvania Railroad, carried his Dreyse Needle gun across the pommel of his saddle as Tate had instructed. Clifton Burge, the self-important back-door relation to Vice President John Breckenridge, was none too happy to be riding with the guide he saw as not only younger than him but beneath him in every standing. Burge preferred to leave his Sharps in the scabbard under the fender of his right stirrup and out of his way. If Tate asked a question or made a comment it was met with one-word answers or ignored completely.

The road had turned on a northwesterly angle and the brilliant oranges of the sunrise came from behind their right shoulder and painted the treetops with muted shades. They were riding into the dim grey of early morning and the shadows stretched into the deeper forest. The stream to the right of the road held tight to the thick brush of Juneberry, chokecherry, and black willow. Sean noted a break in the brush that told of a trail to the water and held out the flat palm to stop Clifton. He motioned to the trail and stepped down from his saddle. He dropped the reins to the ground and with rifle in hand, he signaled to Clifton to follow, but he looked back to see the man struggling to free his Sharps rifle from the scabbard.

Once Burge had his rifle in hand, Sean waited for him to come alongside. He whispered, "I'm pretty sure there's a couple deer at the creek for their morning drink. Go to the edge of the bushes there," he pointed to the tuft of brush that extended out from the rest, "and take a look. If you have a shot, take it." Burge nodded his head and started at a full upright walk to the designated point with Sean watching and shaking his head. The man stopped at the end of the brush, looked around, and brought his rifle to his shoulder and instantly pulled the trigger. Sean saw the two deer scamper up the opposite bank while Burge stood watching.

Sean walked up beside the man, looked at the creek, the opposite bank with the fresh tracks of the scampering deer, and back at Clifton Burge. "Well, it was a long shot!" whined the collegiate. Sean looked again at the scene, guessed the distance to be no more than twenty yards and looked back at Burge. Without saying a word, Sean turned to retrieve their mounts and stepped aboard, waiting for Burge to replace his rifle in the scabbard and get aboard.

Once mounted, he snatched at the reins, pulling his horse's head up with a jerk, and snarled at Sean, "I suppose you could have made that shot?"

Sean just looked at the man with a sidelong glance, saying nothing.

"Well, they jumped!"

Sean nodded his head and gigged his horse forward. He

knew with the big boom of the Sharps rifle, they wouldn't see another deer for several miles and he took the crossing to go back to the roadway. As they neared the road, Sean saw his pa hanging the carcass of a deer from a big branch near, and easily visible from, the road.

When Tate saw the frown on his son's face, he answered, "I took him with my bow. Somethin' you might consider yourself. We're not too far south of Lawrence and Topeka and we might run into some Jayhawkers, so if we can keep 'em from knowin' we're around, all the better."

Clifton asked, "So, just what is a Jayhawker and why should we care if they know we're around?" His question was directed to Tate, who looked to Sean who shrugged his shoulders, telling Tate of his son's disgust with the man in his charge.

Tate finished with hanging the carcass, stepped to the side of Shady, his grulla, and looked at the impertinent questioner. "Jayhawkers or Redlegs are organized groups of free staters that are determined for Kansas to come into the Union as a free state. On the other side are Bushwhackers or Ruffians that want to see it as a slave state. There have been a lot of fights because of the different ideas and folks have been killed. They see any groups of wagons like ours and they are immediately suspicious of our intent. Jayhawkers will stop anyone they think will add to the numbers of slavers, and vice versa. And they'll stop at nothing to keep their side in the majority."

"Well, surely they wouldn't shoot anyone over such a trivial idea, would they?"

"They would, and they have. The battle of Osawatomie, back a couple years, was the worst so far. I think there was something like 25 or so died in that fight. But there's been enough fightin' to know it could get bloody. That's why they call this Bleeding Kansas. And slavery is not now, nor has it ever been a 'trivial idea.'"

Louis Reale, still sitting in his saddle, looked at Tate with a bland expression, believing the remark was directed at him as a slave owner. He chose to keep his silence and waited for Tate to mount up and lead off. Reale looked at Burge with a scowl as if to warn him to keep his remarks to himself. Burge nodded his understanding and the four rode together with the rising sun warming their right shoulders.

They had gone a short distance when Tate motioned Sean forward and the two spoke softly as they rode together. "Son, I'm thinkin' we might be in for a scrap this mornin', the hair on my neck is standin' up and gettin' my attention."

"Me too, Pa. I thought it was just cuz o' that knothead back there, but I think you're right. Things just ain't right."

"Ummhumm. So, you take the knothead and stay in the trees on that side o' the road, back about fifty to a hunert yards, an' we'll do the same on this side. If there's anybody layin' for trouble or come down the road toward the wagons, you know what to do."

Sean nodded his head and reined his Appaloosa off the road, signaling Burge to follow. Once into the trees, Sean reined up and looked to the man. "Did you reload?"

Burge looked down, trying to remember, lifted his eyes, "No, no, I didn't. It's not safe to carry a loaded weapon!" he declared, trying to justify his oversight.

"Load it!" directed Sean.

"Now, see here, young man. How dare you order me like that!"

Sean lifted his eyes to the trees, drew a deep breath, looked directly at the man, "Either do what I tell you, when I tell you, or hightail your skinny little rump back to the wagons and crawl up into your bedroll and hide!"

"Well, humph. Since you put it that way!" He reached for his rifle and brought it to rest across his legs.

Sean knew the mechanics of loading a Sharps and knew it could easily be done while they rode and gigged his horse forward.

Burge said, "Aren't you going to wait?"

"Load it while we ride," ordered Sean over his shoulder without pausing.

The man struggled a little but soon had the paper cartridge inserted and the breech closed. He looked up at Sean and called, "Wait!"

Sean reined up and turned in his saddle to await the man but when he came near, Sean hissed at him, "From here on out, be absolutely quiet! We might be runnin' into some trouble and it would be best if they did not know where we were!"

Wide-eyed, the man looked around the trees, bending to see under some of the branches, and searching all around. He whispered, "I don't see anybody!"

Sean answered in a whisper as he gigged his horse forward, "You better hope you don't!"

LESS THAN AN HOUR LATER, Tate pulled to a stop in a thick grove of trees and stepped down. He motioned to Reale to step down and hold the horses. "I'm goin' to the edge of the trees an' have a look see. I smelled some dust an' I think there might be a bunch a riders and I'd like to see what they're up to. You wait here and whatever you do, don't move or make a sound. Got it?"

"I understand."

"You might have that fancy rifle o'yourn handy too," directed Tate, nodding toward the rifle scabbard.

Reale lifted his head and nodded, reaching for the rifle.

Both Tate and Sean had chosen to carry their Spencers with a pocketful of cartridges on this day and Tate now moved quietly into the trees, rifle cradled in his arms but at the ready. Without even a whisper of his movement, Tate was soon behind a tall, wide oak within a few feet of the road. He climbed into the massive tree, sending Lobo to hide in the thicker trees. With a wide branch for a seat, he could watch the roadway without being seen,

Within moments, the clatter of hooves on the hard-packed dirt told of the approach of several riders. Two men were side-by-side in the lead and were talking loud enough for Tate to hear most of what was said, and he listened as he watched and counted.

"Lige said he figgered at least a dozen wagons, most freighters but several covered wagons. He said he saw some Negras by the fire last night, but he din't know how many they was."

"Well, we'll just have to see 'bout that. We got us 'nuff men to search them wagons and take any o' their slaves. I'm tired o' them southerners tryin' to settle in Kansas an' bringin' their slaves! No sir!"

"Now, Morris, don't go gettin' your dander up. We ain't had to kill nobody so far an' we ain't lost none of our'n. So, we'll just take 'em, but be ready, cuz ya' just don't know. But it won't do anybody any good if you go flyin' off the handle like you been known to do!"

The talkers had passed by and Tate could no longer hear them, but he knew they were going after the wagons. As soon as the rest of the group, which Tate numbered at about fifteen, had passed, he slipped to the ground and trotted back to the horses, Lobo at his heels.

A simple hand wave told Reale to mount up and Tate was

quickly in his saddle and starting toward the road. As expected, he saw Sean coming from the trees and Tate motioned his son and charge to stay on that side but move at the same pace. Tate was about twenty feet to the side of the road and Reale about the same distance away and closer to the trees. Sean and Burge were positioned similarly on the opposite side. Both of the collegians had been told to do exactly as the scouts did, but not before. The four men rode with rifles across their pommels and expectation written on their faces.

Within less than half a mile, the Jayhawkers had fanned out to block the road to the approaching wagons. What they didn't expect was for those of the wagons to be ready for just such an event. When the leaders of the Jayhawkers held their rifles overhead to signal the wagons to stop, John Richards directed his wagons to draw closer before stopping.

To the surprise of the Jayhawkers, the lead wagon stopped, but two freighters pulled to each side of the lead wagon, with roustabouts holding rifles. Once stopped, team-sters lifted their rifles from the wagon seat. Now they faced ten men, rifles ready.

Yet, as is often true with would-be leaders of men that have had some success, the leaders of the Jayhawkers still thought they had the upper hand with experienced fighters against mule skinners. The leader, a man known as Nicode-mus, shouted his bravado, "We're gonna search your wagons! We know you got some slaves an' this is a free state an' we're gonna take them slaves!"

John Richards looked at the man, reached into his jacket pocket and extracted a skinny cigar. He bit off the end, spat it out, and put the cigar in his mouth. He took a lucifer, struck it on the steel concho of his saddle, and lit the cigar. After exhaling the smoke slowly, he then looked at the Jayhawker leader and answered, "No, you ain't!" He hadn't spoken very loudly, but was still heard by the leader.

"You can't stop us! We are the law in this country!"

"No, you ain't! And we won't stop you, we'll just kill you!" Richards had seen the quiet approach of Tate and company behind the Jayhawkers and with a nod of his head, Tate understood. A big boom thundered from behind the men, startling every one of them, and the horse of the leader that had been burnt by the slug from Tate's Spencer set about doing his best to unseat his rider. With no more than a couple of back arching bucks, the horse succeeded in launching his unsuspecting rider over his head to land in a pile in front of his men. The men had been searching the trees for the source of the shot and spotted the four men behind them and with rifles trained on them. The Jayhawkers lowered their own weapons, several slipping their rifles into their scabbards, so there would be no mistake as to their intentions.

Richards rode up to the man that was now crumpled on the ground, watched and waited as he struggled to his feet. John leaned on his pommel and asked, "You were saying?"

Nicodemus stood, brushed himself off, and lifted his eyes to Richards, "This changes nothing! We want your slaves!"

"Friend, I don't think you understand. Now let me help you. I'm a trader from the territories and we're just passing through your Kansas territory. . What we have or don't have is none of your concern and you're not looking into any one of my wagons. And in case you didn't get the message, my men have fought Comanche, Pawnee, Sioux, and more, and your piddlin' little bunch o' farmers don't scare us in the least!" He looked around to see one of the Jayhawkers holding the reins on the leader's horse and added, "Now, why don't you just get on your horse and take your men back home?"

The leader's friend and companion, Morris, who had been the outspoken one overheard by Tate, spurred his horse forward, his hand on his rifle that lay across the pommel. He moved his mount so the rifle was pointed in the general direction of Richards without threatening. But Morris spoke angrily, "Mister, this is a free state and you have no right bringing slaves into it, now we're gonna take 'em!"

Richards leaned forward, his left hand holding the reins and his right resting on the saddle horn, but fingers reaching toward the pistol at his waist that was obscured by his jacket. "Friend, you're wrong on all counts. This ain't a state yet, much less a free state, and I can bring whatever or whoever I want with me and there ain't a thing you can do about it. Now if you know what's good for you, you'll back off and go home." Richards spoke through gritted teeth and his expression was as stern as his voice was firm. .

Morris narrowed his eyes, sucked several short breaths, and started to move his rifle towards Richards. The pistol spat flame and smoke and the three shots sounded almost as one as the Colt Dragoon .44 roared. Morris was struck with every shot and almost lifted from his saddle as wide eyes stared in fear and shock at his shooter. He slumped forward, losing his grip on the rifle that clattered to the ground, and he fell atop the weapon, his horse shying away. Blood blossomed on the back of the man's jacket and the entire group of Jayhawkers stared in shock.

Richards turned the Dragoon on Nicodemus, and with a low voice said, "That was your fault. Now pick up your friend and take your men home like I said."

Nicodemus looked up at Richards, nodded his head and motioned to a nearby man to help. Within moments they had the body draped over the horse and without looking back, the crowd of Jayhawkers, heads hanging, took the road back the direction they came.

Richards breathed deep, holstered his Dragoon, and motioned the wagons back on the road. He waited for Tate to come near, asked, "You saw?"

"Ummhumm. Couldn't be helped."

"Don't make it any easier, though."

"Nope." The two men rode together as they led the wagons toward the distant river crossing.

IT WAS JUST ENOUGH OF A KNOLL TO OVERLOOK THE meandering Big Blue River below. Father and son watched as the brilliant oranges and golds of the setting sun bounced off the waters and gave the day a serene finish. Two days past the wagons made the ferry crossing of the Kansas River and the journey north had been easy and uneventful. The comfortable camp with the wagons circled up and the animals enjoying the graze of tall spring grass, offered the travelers a restful stop before the crossing of the Big Blue River.

Tate and Sean had a simple supper of fresh venison steaks broiled over the fire and a fried vegetable medley of morel mushrooms, asparagus, and cat-tail root. They sat near the fire nursing the hot coffee, both staring into the flames and lost in their thoughts. Sean looked to his father and asked, "Missin' Ma, are ya?"

Tate let a chuckle escape and answered, "I was just rememberin' our trek out here. Your ma and I got us a couple bucks just across the river yonder. That's where we spotted the Jayhawkers as they crossed the river hereabouts."

"You didn't have that look on your face cuz you were thinkin' 'bout Jayhawkers."

"No, you're right. And I'm sure there's gonna be lotsa times when I'm missin' your ma, but this is important for your sister." He tossed a stick into the flames, watched the sparks rise to the treetops and added, "But we've got a bunch o' pilgrims to nursemaid for a few months . . ."

"Have you noticed there's a couple of 'em that haven't gone out scoutin' with us?"

"Yeah, them two always seem to still be in their bedrolls when we head out, an' there's always two others that are ready to go. I think I heard one o' the others call one of 'em Malcolm somethin'."

"Mebbe we need to latch onto 'em when we stop for noonin' or sumpin'," suggested Sean, looking to his father across the fire.

"I have noticed they seem to always be travelin' together on the wagons. Leastways one or the other drives the wagon so they're learnin' sumpin'. Oh well, let's turn in, we've gotta get these wagons across first thing so we can make some time tomorrow. If we have a good day, we'll be outta Bleedin' Kansas and be hittin' the Oregon Trail soon."

THE RISING sun was at their backs and stretched their shadows before them as they rolled off the knoll toward the low water with the gravel bottom.. This was the first real river crossing for the pilgrims handling the covered wagons and it would be nothing like riding the ferry over the Kansas River. The four covered wagons rotated their position at the start of every day but always stayed ahead of the bigger freighters handled by the more experienced teamsters. The college men had buddied up and two were in each wagon, and each carried one of the servants.

Richards had asked Tate and Sean to ride alongside the wagons in case any of them got into trouble, to which Tate responded, "Trouble? That water ain't but stirrup deep. What trouble could they get into?"

"Who knows? But if there's some to be found, they'll find it!"

The crossing was on the Big Blue just before the confluence with the Little Blue River. Once across the wagons would follow the Little Blue north into Nebraska Territory to the headwaters before joining the Oregon Trail by the Platte River. Tate knew there was always the danger of quicksand, especially when the river bottom shifted and bent back on itself. This crossing started with a wide sandbar before dropping into the slow current and across the gravelly bottom to the opposite shore. It was not a difficult crossing and he thought it should go without incident.

Tate sat in the saddle, leaning forward with his elbows resting on the pommel as he watched the wagons descend the knoll and approach the riverbank where he waited. He saw the first wagon was driven by Malcolm Whitehurst, one of the two that had ducked out on the hunting ventures, and the seat was shared by his friend, Erastus Throckmorton. Tate didn't know their full names, the earlier introductions were strictly first names, but he was also pleased to see the old slave Jeremiah standing behind the young men.

Tate nodded his head as they neared, sat up in the saddle, "Alright fellas," he said with his hand upheld to stop them. "This is an easy crossing. I'll be riding beside you but all you need to do," he nodded toward the driver who was on the right side of the wagon seat, "is keep 'em movin'. Can you handle that?" he pointed toward the buggy whip that stood in a crack beside the seat.

"Uh, yessir," answered Malcom, reaching for the whip to stand it in the front corner of the box.

"Good. Sometimes the mules get a little skittish, mebbe see a cottonmouth or a floatin' stick that skeers 'em. But all ya gotta do is crack that whip o'er their heads or even smack 'em on the rump to keep 'em movin'. Ya' don't wanna stop in the middle of the river. Got that?"

"Uh, I think so," answered an obviously nervous Malcolm. Tate noticed the second man, Erastus, holding tight to the end of the wagon seat with his knuckles turning white and his eyes wide. Tate thought, *Uh Oh, he's gonna be trouble.*

"Now, when you get to the other side, you might have to use the whip again so they'll pull up the bank and get the wagon outta the river." He looked at the men, glanced at Jeremiah who was grinning and trying to keep from laughing, and then motioned for them to follow.

Tate leaned back against his cantle as Shady stepped easily down the bank to the sandbar. He waited until the wagon was beside him and they started into the water together. The front wheels of the wagon had just entered the water when Tate looked to see Erastus tensing up and looking at the murky water splashing against the wheels. The nervous man's eyes grew wider as Tate stayed near, watching.

Once the wagon was in the water, the current caught the bottom of the box and the wagon rocked. That slight rock made Erastus lean forward and put a hand over his mouth as he stared at the rushing water. The mules were pulling at a steady pace, picking their footing, but showing no alarm. The driver was on the upstream side and often looked to the water and the stream coming at them. He saw a gnarly branch floating in the water and said, "Oh my, it's a cottonmouth!"

Erastus leaned forward to look, jumped to his feet to see better, and screamed. He put his hand on the shoulders of Malcolm, who was reaching for the whip, stepped to the seat and grabbed at the bow holding the canvas top, and was dancing back and forth from one foot to the other. He stuttered, held one hand to his mouth, looked down at the water and started screaming, "We're gonna die! We're gonna die! We're gonna die!"

Tate had watched everything and struggled to keep from busting out laughing, but when the man started screaming, he knew he had to do something before the mules spooked. Moving Shady closer to the wagon, he stood in his stirrups and grabbed the shirt of Erastus and pulled him from the seat, jerked him over his horse and dropped him into the water. Tate watched as he splashed and sputtered, trying to scream for help. Malcolm stood to see where his friend went and looked at Tate, shouting "He'll drown! Help him!"

"You help him!" ordered Tate.

The man had a loose grip on the reins but was leaning over the edge of the wagon to search for his friend. He looked up at Tate and shouted again, "Help him!"

Tate grabbed the man's collar and snatched him from the seat and dropped him into the muddy water just a couple feet from his floundering friend. He looked to Jeremiah, "Take the wagon on across, I'll tend to them."

The big slave was laughing as he climbed over the back of the seat, picked up the lead lines and the whip to crack the popper over the heads of the mules shouting, "Get along Mule, Git!"

Tate turned back to the panicked men, watched them splashing toward one another and hollered, "Stand up!"

Malcolm scowled at the man in the saddle as he continued splashing in his panic fit, and heard another shout from Tate "Stand up!"

Malcolm stretched his legs down, searching for footing with his toes, struck the bottom and slowly stood. The water was no deeper than the bottom of his rib cage and he shook his head as he reached out a hand for the sputtering Erastus, and shouted, "Stand up!"

Once both men were standing, Tate turned Shady toward the shore, but not after seeing the approaching second wagon. Sitting in the seat were Patrick and Justis, both laughing and pointing at their friends in the water. Sean grinned as he reined his Appaloosa past the waterlogged two and pointed to the far sand bar for the wagon driven by Patrick.

The rest of the wagons crossed without incident and the train didn't stop for the usual nooning, wanting to put as many miles behind them as possible and hopefully make it into Nebraska Territory. But the dusk dimmed the trail and Tate and Sean picked a cove of a wide meadow where a small stream fought its way to merge with the Little Blue. Near the river was a sizable farmhouse and before they went to camp, Tate and Sean stopped at the farm to talk to the man that watched from his rail fence.

"Evenin'," said Tate as he neared the fence. "We've got some wagons comin' up the trail and thought we'd camp over yonder by the trees. That be alright with you?"

"Free country! I ain't rightly claimed that field yet, might someday, but I got 'nuff to do without addin' to it. Goin' fer are ye?" asked the man, tucking his thumbs under his galluses. His chin whiskers bobbed with every word as did the foxtail weed between his teeth.

"Rocky Mountains eventually but won't make it today," drawled Tate as he leaned on the pommel.

"Nope, don't reckon. Say, if'n you're needin' any groceries or supplies, I got muh barn purty well stocked." He nodded back toward the buildings and Tate noticed the big barn standing behind the farmhouse.

"Looks like you been doin' some building. Got yourself a right nice place here."

"Thankee, thankee. What with all the wagons like your'n comin' through, I thought I'd set up a general store of sorts. And what with Waddell and company haulin' supplies to the western forts, they come through here purt' regular and just th' other day, had a feller name o' Majors say they're gonna partner up with Waddell an' start some kinda mail service an' they wanted to have me set up a station fer 'em, with bunks an' such. Gettin' plumb civilized roun' chere."

Tate shook his head, looked to Sean, back to the farmer, "And your name is . . . ?"

"Hollenberg, Geret Hollenberg. Don't ferget, need any groceries an' such, come on back!"

Tate watched as the man turned his back and started trudging through the newly cultivated field, picking his steps carefully, but with the recognizable gait of a farmer. Sean spoke up, "Just can't get back to the mountains soon enough!"

Tate snorted as he started to chuckle, "That's for sure!"

They rode back to the wide meadow, flagged the wagons and pointed them to the campsite. Tate thought about the excitement of earlier in the day and wondered just what the conversation would be around the campfire tonight.

CHAPTER FIFTEEN
NEBRASKA

SEAN POKED AT THE COALS, STIRRING THEM TO LIFE AS A TINY flame licked at the splintered wood recently placed atop the smoldering remnants. The lad added more kindling until the hungry fire flared, asking for more. The greyed wood of the broken branches sated the appetite of the dancing flames and Sean pushed the freshly filled coffeepot to the edge of the flat rock. He knew his pa would soon return from his moments of solitude and prayer and his eyes would scan the campsite for Maggie, as she so often would be there to welcome him to the new day. But today there would only be Sean, a bit long-faced, perhaps, but just as happy to see his pa.

Sean sat back on the smooth log that served as both bench and breakfast table and glanced toward the treeline where his father had walked as the stars dimmed their lanterns and bid their adieu to the rising sun. Although the golden orb had yet to rise above the black horizon, the darkness that was so bold just moments ago now bowed its head in retreat. Sean lifted his eyes to the treetops as the dim grey light of early morning began to give color once again to the monotonous landscape of leafy trees, grassy meadows, and low rolling hills. He thought of his mountains and how he longed for the horizon that held the granite fingers that clawed at the blue skies and the towering pines that filled the air with a freshness only found in the high lonesome. Sean breathed deep in the memories of the wilderness, then looked around and beyond to the camp of the wagons. He saw the stirring of life among them and noted the only ones moving near the covered wagons were the four slaves who were busy about the usual morning chores.

He thought of the group of men that he and his pa were guiding, and he considered them as a group and as individuals. They were so different than any men he had known, and he had spent the last several days observing and listening. Their attitude towards others was what his ma would have described as arrogant and disdainful. Patrick Hutton had told Tate that he thought his life and those of his friends was of more value than those less privileged. . The one that his pa had thrown into the water looked down on everyone with an attitude of superiority, like others should kowtow to him. Sean chuckled as he remembered the look on the man's face when he floundered in the shallow water, thinking he was going to drown.

Yet it seemed that all of the group thought themselves above those of the wagon train. Maybe it was because they came from families of influence and money, or perhaps they were lacking in understanding of the real worth of people. Sean shook his head as he pondered these men. Although younger than the collegians, he didn't feel any less of a man in their presence, but they continually tried to exert some kind of dominance over him. Maybe it was because of his youth, or what they perceived as their better education, but Sean thought it was just a normal insolence for them, perhaps learned from their homelife. Pa had said that 'the apple doesn't fall far from the tree' and that when the parents had the attitude of narcissism, the children will naturally assume a similar demeanor.

Sean remembered the words of his father, "It's a shame when that happens, son, because I was always taught that a man has to make his own way in this world. It's not what his name is, or the home he comes from, or even how much wealth he may have, it's what he makes of himself that counts. Now these fellas, they're out here on their own for the first time in their lives and they're clinging to the past, what they were in college or at home, but those things don't mean much out here. That's what they're beginning to understand, and it will only become clearer in the days ahead. You'll see some of 'em learn and grow, and others will hold on to the past for all its worth and they'll have to learn some mighty hard lessons, and the pity is, some of 'em won't learn a thing."

Sean stood to stretch and saw the camp below was stirring a little more, but the camp of the college men, or pilgrims as his pa called them, was the same. Only the slaves were moving about preparing the breakfast and coffee for the group while they still lay abed. Sean wondered if the men would starve for lack of someone waiting on them? He chuckled to himself, stirred the coals again and pulled the coffee pot back from the flames. He scraped the fresh grounds from the flat rock into his palm, removed the lid from the pot and dropped them into the steaming water. He pushed the pot back closer to the flames when he heard the soft footfalls, "Mornin' Pa," he said without turning.

"Mornin' son," Tate answered as he walked to the edge of the fire, extending his hands for the warmth. "I think just you n' me'll go on the scout this mornin'. We'll let them high-water-britches boys have a day off, so they can pout an' lick their wounds a little. We'll be gettin' into Pawnee country later today an' I'd just as soon not have to worry 'bout them city kids and what they might do if we run up on some o' those 'savages' they're so concerned about."

"Sounds fine to me, Pa. I think I'd rather spend time with the 'savages' than that bunch o' sissy britches!"

PATRICK HUTTON WAS the first one to roll out of his blankets and stick his head out of the canvas bonnet of the wagon. He smelled the coffee and heard the sizzle of the pork belly in the frying pan and he reached over the shake Justis awake. "C'mon sleepyhead! We gotta get a move on before ol' Richards comes around and threatens to leave us behind!" He climbed from the wagon, holding his boots and britches in one hand as he stepped to the ground. Leaning against the wheel, he pulled on his wool britches, tucked in the linen shirttail, drew the galluses over his shoulders and reached for his boots. He stomped his feet into the high-topped boots and started for the woods for his morning constitutional. Justis followed close behind.

When they returned to the fire, the others were crawling from their wagons and following suit as their self-appointed leader called out, "C'mon you lazies! Get a move on! You're gonna miss breakfast!"

His announcement was met with the usual grumbling and complaining as the other men staggered around in stages of undress trying to get ready for the day. Patrick accepted a plate of pork belly and grits and a cup of steaming coffee from Timothy, the youngest of the slaves, and nodded his appreciation. It was not an acceptable manner to express gratitude to a slave, but Patrick was not from a slave-holding family. Even though he was loud and obnoxious and some-what pompous, he knew that was mostly put-on, because he was rapidly learning what it was to be a real man. That scout,

Tate, was beginning to grow on him and his respect for the man was taking hold.

Malcolm Whitehurst and Erastus Throckmorton came to the fire, neither was in cheerful mood and both grumbled when they took their plates and cups from the slave, Johnathan. They sat silently as they downed their meal and when finished they, in an expression of their brewing anger, threw the tin plates toward the table where the slaves worked. Malcolm stood, "How long are we going to put up with their insolence?" he demanded, pointing toward the scouts and looking from one to the other of his companions. "Well?" he asked again, standing with arms outstretched toward the group.

Patrick stood, "Just what do you expect?"

"They need to be put in their place! They're nothing but hirelings and they need to show respect to their betters! What he did yesterday was totally disrespectful and demeaning, and I, for one, will not stand for it!" he shouted, stomping a foot into the ground like a child throwing a fit.

"And exactly how are *you* going to teach them to *respect their betters?*" asked Justis, looking at Patrick and back to the protestors.

"Well, uh, well, they should be horsewhipped!" he demanded, nodding his head toward his friend, Erastus, who nodded in agreement.

Patrick sat his coffee cup on the tailgate to the wagon, turned slowly to face the complainer, "Malcolm, if Tate hadn't thrown you into the water, you'd still be standing in the wagon screaming like a little girl! If he hadn't done what he did, you would have spooked the mules and caused who knows what kind of damage."

"But, but, he didn't need to throw Erastus in also!" he whined.

"Look," said Patrick, and motioned to the rest of the

group, "we all know you're a crybaby and 'Rastus too, and it's high time you knew the only reason we allowed you to come is because your Mommy is paying for it all. Now, I suggest you grow up a bit and learn what Tate and Sean have to teach us. I'm thinkin' we can all learn a good deal!"

Malcolm stuttered and stammered as the others turned away and began the preparations to get under way. Erastus put his arm around his friend's shoulder, "Malcolm, my friend, we'll just have to handle things our own way. These ruffians have no idea who they're dealing with, and even though your mother is paying the way, I, for one, am very glad we are on this grand adventure together."

FOUR DAYS of uneventful travel saw the pilgrims from Yale keeping to themselves. Tate and Sean did not solicit their presence on the scouts nor did the pilgrims ask to accompany the guides on any hunts. From the outset of the trip, Tate had understood it to be Richards' responsibility to see to the care and keeping of the easterners, at least until they departed Fort Bernard for the actual buffalo hunt. Yet, Tate had noticed a few of the young men casting glances his way whenever they were in camp, but he thought nothing of it until Patrick visited the camp of the scouts.

"May I join you?" asked the only one of the group that Tate thought had some potential as a man.

"Of course, we're just enjoyin' some coffee, care for some?" answered Tate, reaching for the pot.

Patrick seated himself on a stump near the fire, accepted the offered cup of java and took a quick sip of the black brew then lifted his eyes to Tate. "How's the hunting?"

"Oh, good 'nuff. Bringin' in some meat on a regular basis keeps the teamsters happy and limits the complainin', course there's always gonna be grumbling anytime you have hard work involved."

"Humm, and since you mention complaining, I thought I oughta tell you something. After you gave Malcolm and 'Rastus their well-deserved dunking, they've been doin' a little conspiring together and I'm not comfortable with what I've been hearing."

"Oh, and what's that?" asked Tate, curious but not concerned.

"You have to understand those two, you see, it's Malcolm's father that thought of this trip and his mother that's paying for it all. Malcolm's father thought, rightly so, that a trip of this sort would help make a man of his son. They're what you call 'old money' and they take great pride in a genealogy that boasts of nobility and kinship to royalty, and they believe they should be treated like royalty. Of course, they're the only ones that believe that, but still, it's an attitude that Malcolm carries. All the way through college he strutted around the campus and refused to involve himself with us commoners," Patrick chuckled as he remembered, "but we accepted him. At least to his willingness to be a part of our group. And, when this opportunity knocked, the rest of us thought it would be a grand adventure."

"I see, but what does all that have to do with us?" asked Tate as he motioned to Sean and himself.

"Well, what I've been picking up on, is they think they need to teach you some manners and respect, at least as far as Malcolm is concerned. Now, I don't know how or when they think they're going to do whatever they've got planned, but I thought it best if you knew what they were thinking."

Tate dropped his eyes to the fire, looked back to Patrick, "I really hate to hear that. Those boys don't know what kind of trouble that can cause, we're not in what you fellas call 'civilization' and if they do something careless or dangerous, the consequences could be deadly. You see, there's no constable on the corner, no judge in the courthouse, and no parents he can go running to because out here the only law is what good people make it and that doesn't mean a trial with a jury of your peers. It's usually at the end of a rope or weighted with lead and there are few second chances."

"I understand, and I hope it won't come to that," resolved Patrick, tossing the dregs of his coffee away.

He started to leave when Tate stood, offered his hand, and cautioned, "It might help if you talk to him."

"We've tried, but his dander is up, and he's determined."

AFTER PATRICK LEFT, Sean asked, "So, what do you think is gonna happen?"

"Son, it's hard to tell what might happen. When somebody like Malcolm, who is used to folks catering to his every whim and never having to take responsibility for his own misbehavior, has to face up to things, it can be a bitter pill for them to swallow. He's got some hard lessons to learn and I hope he graduates from the school of experience before he gets somebody hurt or killed." He picked up a stick, added it to the fire, looked to Sean, "We will just have to be extra careful 'bout everything. You can't predict what someone bent on vengeance might do or when they'll do it. So, just be extra careful 'bout everything."

"I understand Pa, but for right now, I'm turnin' in cuz my blankets are beckoning."

THE FOUR DAYS TRAVEL TO THE PLATTE RIVER IN NEBRASKA Territory had given Tate and Sean the opportunity to hunt and talk together. Seldom camping with the wagons, the two scouts stayed well ahead of the train, leaving their meat kills hanging near the road for the men to find. The one issue that seemed to trouble Sean the most was slavery. "I guess I just don't understand, Pa. How do the slaves allow themselves to become slaves, can't they just get up an' leave?"

Tate was quiet for a few moments then started doing his best to explain, "I know it's not the best way to explain it, but, think about your horse, or Indy and Lobo. Each of them was wild and on their own, free to go wherever they wanted, but along comes man. With a horse, man captures 'em, keeps 'em penned up, and begins to break their spirit and tames them. Then he works with 'em to train 'em to do what he wants. With Lobo, it was different, because I gave him shelter and food, he grew to like me and stays with me, like a friend. In both cases, what they knew before has changed and they become dependent on the man that feeds them.

"But in the case of man and slaves, the slavers have gone

further and added severe punishment if the slave tries to escape. Often, he's beaten, whipped, starved, and more, until his spirit is replaced with fear. If he escapes, he's tracked down and punished and sometimes the punishment is to torture his loved ones as well. That takes a lot out of a man and as most men do even in other circumstances, they choose the only way they can see to survive, and they remain slaves."

"I couldn't do it, Pa. If somebody tried to make me a slave, I'd never give in, I'd fight as long as I had the strength," he paused, thinking, "Maybe that's one of the reasons I like it in the mountains, ya' don't see all this slavery stuff."

Tate looked at his son, "There's slavery in the mountains as well, just not quite the same as you've seen it here. There have been many times different tribes have taken captives and made slaves out of them. That's been goin' on longer than the slavery of the black man you've seen out here. Wherever there's been men, there's been slaves, even back in Bible times."

"Still ain't right," grumbled Sean.

As they neared the Platte, they pushed through the meadow grass and fields of blue and purple flowers that grew so high the blooms touched the bottoms of their stirrups. A break in the thick foliage offered access to the river and Sean noted an unusual bush with a flower that looked like a small white ball with stickers. He shook his head at the marvelous abundance and contrasts the territory held.

Suddenly Tate reined up, causing the Appaloosa to bump into the rear of Shady. Sean lifted his eyes to see Tate staring across the river at what was obviously someone's camp. Seated on a log near a smoldering fire was a man wearing an odd-looking woolen cap with a ball of something on top. He puffed on a bent-stem pipe that protruded from under a thick moustache that drooped to his chin whiskers. He was looking their way and waved for them to join him. Tate gigged Shady into the shallow sandy-bottomed river, followed closely by Sean, to make their way across the slow-moving stream. They rose from the streambed, paused as the horses did their usual rolling shake to rid their bellies and legs of the water, then walked their mounts to the campsite.

The man on the log moved only his free hand to motion for his visitors to dismount and join him at the fire. He puffed on his pipe, emitting a small cloud of blue-grey smoke, and broadened his face into a barely perceptible smile that showed only in his eyes. His rifle lay to his side, but his hands were otherwise occupied as he reached for the coffee pot and asked, "You like coffee, no?" His accent was new to Sean, and his attire was different, with woolen britches tucked into tall laced boots, a simple dark shirt was rumpled under his galluses, and his woolen cap caught Sean's eye as he tried to make out what the ball on the top was made from.

Tate took his tin cup from the tie beside the cantle and walked to the fire. He stepped over a log that lay opposite the fire from the camper and extended his cup for the man to fill it with the black brew. When the man lifted the pot toward Sean, the extended cup was filled, and Sean sat beside his father.

"I see, you are father and son, no?" asked the man, grinning.

Tate nodded, "That's right. I'm Tate and this is my son, Sean."

"*Oui*, I see. I am Jacques Bottineau, from the Red River country, far to the north."

"French?" asked Tate.

"My father was French, my mother, Clear Sky Woman, was Dakota and Ojibwe. We are called Métis."

"I reckon the 'we' you refer to are those two in the trees with rifles pointed at us?" asked Tate, nonchalantly.

Bottineau chuckled, dropped his eyes from Tate and motioned with an arm over his head for the rifle holders to come back to the fire. Tate and Sean were surprised to see two women come from the trees with rifles held at their hips and pointed at the visitors. . Neither woman smiled nor looked away from the visitors. One was older, perhaps thirty-five or forty years, and the other was nearer Sean's age. Both were clad in buckskin tunics over leggings that were adorned with fringe, trade ornaments, and beads, not unlike most native women of the plains. They stood on either side of the man and waited for his words, which he quickly spoke in a smattering of languages that neither Tate nor Sean could understand. The women dropped the muzzles of their rifles and sat them down beside the man's.

"This is my wife, *Wakpadoota* or Red Leaf, and my daughter, Reindeer Fawn."

"Reindeer? There are no reindeer here," declared Sean, surprised at his own words, but he had been startled by the beauty of the young woman that held him mesmerized and he didn't realize he had spoken his thoughts out loud. He sat up, trying to act as if he hadn't been bothered, but he dared to sneak a look at the young woman who gave him a coy glance. Long straight hair hung over her shoulders almost to her waist, deep black eyes sparkled from under thin brows. Her high cheekbones framed her narrow nose and full lips, bitten to a pout, parted in a slight smile. Sean dropped his eyes, catching his breath, and squirmed on the log, looking to his father for deliverance. But both his pa and her father grinned at the young man, knowingly.

Jacques responded, "No, but where we are from, there are many reindeer, and the newborn reminded her mother of curiosity of our child and so she was named." The man spoke with a distinctive French accent and was sometimes difficult to understand, but the words came almost as a reprimand to Sean.

The young man said, "I'm sorry, I had no right to question. I was just surprised. I read about the reindeer but have never seen one."

"Ahhh, the world is full of wonders for us to discover, are there not?" asked Bottineau.

"There certainly are and for us, meeting someone like you so far from your native lands is one of those wonders." Tate had noticed several racks with meat drying and a wide stone that had been used for grinding or something and his curiosity was piqued. "You've been camped here a while, and I see you're drying some meat. Is that buffalo?"

"*Mais Oui*, it is," answered Jacques, and having noticed Tate looking at the grinding stones, he added, "And we have been making pemmican as well. Do you travel alone?"

"No, we're scouting for a wagon train that's followin' behind. Well, mostly freighters, but some wagons as well. Headin' out to Fort Bernard and doin' a little buffalo huntin' too."

"I see, but is not the Oregon Trail on the other side of the river?"

"Yes, but this side has become known as the Mormon Trail. The trader, John Richards, thought this time o' the summer there might be more graze for the animals on this side, so, we're gonna give it a try."

"*Oui*, I see. Would the men of your wagons like to buy or trade for some *taureau?* Maybe some *taureaux fins,* or *taureaux grand* or *taureaux à grains?*"

"Maybe, if I knew what you were talkin' 'bout."

"Ahh, pardon me. Uh, *taureau* is a bag of pemmican. *Taureaux fins* is pemmican made with fat from the udder. *Taureaux grand* is pemmican made with bone marrow, and *taureaux à grains* is pemmican with berries."

Tate nodded his head and said, "Ya know, they just might." He stood, looked around and pointed to the open field beyond the trees, "That right there would prob'ly be a good camp for the night an' I'll have our trader, John Richards, come see you 'bout some o' them, what you call it, *taureau?*"

"*Mais oui.*"

"So, is there anything you need me to tell your ma?" asked Tate. As usual, he and Sean were camped apart from the wagons and they sat by their fire as the sun tucked itself behind the far horizon. Maggie had purchased a small leather satchel with writing materials, paper, pens, and ink for Tate. She said, it was so he would have no excuses about writing. Using the dim light of dusk and the glow of the campfire he had used the unfamiliar pen to craft the first letter that he expected to post at the nearby Fort Kearny.

Sean lifted his eyes to his pa, "What? What'd you say?"

Tate chuckled. He had watched the boy staring glassy-eyed at the fire and suspected it had something to do with the Métis girl. "I said, is there anything you want to say to your ma?" motioning with the pen to the paper on the satchel on his lap.

"Uh, no, nothin' I guess," he looked to his pa, "you sure you can post that at the Fort?"

"Ummhumm, I'm thinkin' it's probably the last place with a real message center. They say they've got a stage line that runs through here an' can take letters both ways, east an' west."

"Mmmm, that's good," replied Sean, lapsing back into his pensive state.

Their reverie and solitude were interrupted by a visit from John Richards, "Howdy fellas!"

"Why, hello John. To what do we owe this visit?" asked

Tate, finishing off the letter and folding it to insert it into the envelope. As he addressed the envelope, he looked to Richards with eyebrows raised in a question.

"Oh, I wanted to run somethin' by you, see what you think. I was visiting with Jacques and as I saw all the stuff he was doin' with the buffalo, I thought maybe he might help us."

"Oh?" asked Tate, curious at this new idea of John's.

RICHARDS SUMMARIZED HIS IDEA WITH, "So, IF THEY COME with us, they can use the meat from the buffalo, and teach these youngsters 'bout usin' everything like the natives do, what'dya think?"

"Glad to hear you say that, John. I was a little concerned about the hunt wastin' the meat. I'd thought about gettin' some of the local tribes to join us, but your idea is sound. And from what I've seen so far, I think both Sean and I might learn some things, too."

Tate grinned at his son who dropped his head showing the color coming to the back of his neck. They had talked about the Métis family and the different culture they displayed, and Sean had smiled as John spoke of the family traveling with the wagons.

THE WAGON TRAIN spent a day at Fort Kearny, a collection of wood and adobe structures with no wall or fortifications, resupplying before starting on the long journey across Nebraska Territory into the unorganized territories and to

Fort Bernard, the trading post just a few miles southeast of the better-known Fort Laramie. Fort Kearny had been established as a resupply station for the many wagon trains of settlers moving through and the commander told Tate that he estimated over 5,000 wagons had passed through so far that year. "We've seen more an' now that so many Mormons are comin' through on the north trail, it's hard to count how many o' those handcarts have come along. In the past ten years that this fort has been standin', there's been so many settlers come through, I don't know where they all been goin', an' sometimes I wonder if there's anybody left back east, cuz they just keep comin'!"

"Well, thankfully, most of 'em have kept right on a'goin' to Oregon or California. It's got to be we can't go more'n a month that we don't see some pilgrims or others movin' through. Ain't until ya' get past Laramie that ya' quit seein' new farmhouses croppin' up!" declared Tate, shaking his head.

As SEAN and Tate continued on their scouts, Jacques would often ride with them, leaving his women to tend to the pack-horses and gear. It was late on the third day from Fort Kearny when they crossed the trail of several buffalo. "Ah! Buffalo, but very few, probably stragglers from the migration," declared Jacques as he dropped from his mount to examine the tracks. "I would say, oh, fifteen to twenty, mostly cows and calves, a few bulls." He stood, shaded his eyes to look to the north. "There!" he pointed to a slight knoll and the wide valley to the left. He moved his eyes to the far left, "*Mais Oui!* There is a stream that runs into this one," pointing behind them, "and they are grazing in that valley by the little stream."

Tate lifted his eyes to the lowering sky and the sun

nearing the western horizon, "I don't think this is a good time to go after 'em. What with them clouds looking bad and not much daylight, I think we oughta leave it till mornin'. Don'tchu?"

"*Oui,* to butcher a buffalo is hard, but to do it in the rain and the dark, *pas agréable,* eh, not pleasant!"

"Then, let's be gettin' back to the wagons and get 'em to make camp 'fore this storm hits."

"*Mais Oui,* and since my women will cook the dinner, you and your son must join us!"

"Well, that's right fine of you, Jacques. We'll just do that," answered Tate as he reined Shady around to start back to the wagons. They were about three miles ahead of the wagons and would wait near the trees to signal them to make camp. The men stepped down, let the reins of their mounts drop to the ground and found a seat to wait. Lobo and Indy lay beside the men, enjoying the rest. As the horses grazed, Sean asked, "Jacques, you said you were from the far north, and you mentioned Red River country. I've never been farther north than the Missouri River, and I'm guessing your country is even farther north, am I right?"

"*Oui.* But not only north, east also. Our home country as you call it, is in Canada or the Hudson Bay territory."

Sean grinned, "Oh! I read about the Hudson Bay and I've heard some trappers talk about the Hudson Bay Company. Is there still much trapping up there? Cuz down here, with the low price of beaver pelts, there ain't too many still trapping."

"No, there's not a lot. My people, the Métis, we hunt buffalo and sell our goods to the Hudson Bay Company. We keep what we need, smoke and fix the rest into very good pemmican, and sell it by the *taureau* or bag to the company."

"Seems like a lot o' work to me," responded Sean, shaking his head as he poked at the dirt with a stick.

"*Oui.* It is hard work. But our entire village goes on the

hunts. The last hunt we were on, we had 62 hunters and families, we killed over 2,000 buffalo and hauled the meat and pemmican in 300 Red River Carts. You see, it takes about five pounds of meat to make one pound dried. When the dried meat is pounded and mixed with the marrow or fat or berries, it is two times as heavy and sells for more money. Our people keep and use much of it, but when we trade or sell it for other things like powder and lead and more, it makes our life better."

Sean nodded his head in understanding, remembering when their friends from the Ute and Comanche peoples had taught his mother how to make the pemmican; it was a common practice to smoke much of the meat they took. He also remembered that most of that work was done by the women of the native people and he glanced at Jacques, wondering if it was the same with the Métis.

"Here come the wagons," said Tate as he stood to his feet. The three men mounted and started toward the lead wagon and the riders beside it. As they drew near, they recognized the riders as the women of Jacques' family and he went to their side and began conversing in the language unique to them. Tate looked to Richards who rode on the opposite side of the wagons, "What with those clouds lookin' a little dark, I thought we'd make camp here," he motioned with a swing of his arm toward the tree line. "And, we spotted some buffalo up yonder a ways and thought we'd get us some fresh meat in the morning."

"Umm, fresh buffalo sounds mighty fine. We've eaten so much deer meat I was thinking I was growin' antlers!" answered a grinning Richards.

"Does that mean we'll get to do some buffalo hunting?" asked an eager Patrick from the wagon seat. He and his usual sidekick Justis were on the seat of the lead wagon and both looked expectantly to Tate.

"We might take a couple of you with us. Don't need more'n a couple buffalo to feed this crew, but we might take three or four. Jacques could teach some of you how to butcher the buffalo and what to do with all the meat. Be good education for you fellas."

The two looked to one another, and grinned as they nodded to Tate, hopeful of being selected to go on the hunt.

TATE AND SEAN usually made their camp away from the wagons, and Jacques and his family had taken to camping near the scouts. None of the small group was accustomed to larger crowds and were more comfortable in the small camp. Sean and Fawn had not spoken to one another, but neither missed an opportunity to be near and to help one another in the camp chores.

Red Leaf and Fawn prepared a fine meal of boiled meat with some fried leafy greens of the dandelion and stinging nettle. Some shoots of the cat-tail were added to late growing asparagus and morel mushrooms to flavor the pot with the meat.

Everyone ate heartily and as they sat back for a cup of coffee, Red Leaf spoke quietly to Jacques and the conversation obviously upset him. He breathed deeply and looked to Tate, "I must speak to you about something." He cleared his voice and sat up straight, making a noticeable attempt to control himself. "Today, as we rode to scout, two of the young men from the wagons rode by my women and tried to talk to them. The words they used were, how you say, *non conforme*, uh, improper. They believed my women could not understand what they say, and they were very rude." Red Leaf and Fawn sat together, apart from the men, but near, and both hung their heads.

Tate shook his head and asked, "Do they know who it was that spoke to them?" Tate addressed his question to Jacques.

Jacques looked to his wife, eyebrows raised in a question and nodding his head. Red Leaf looked to Tate and in concise English answered, "I believe they called each other Malcolm and Rastus? Is that right?" she looked to Fawn as she questioned the name.

Fawn nodded her head to agree, then added, "They laughed a lot at what they said, but we did not let them know we understood. It is not proper to speak to men we do not know."

Jacques interjected, "We," motioning to himself and his women, "all speak several languages, French, English, Dakota, Ojibwe, and others as well as sign language. Usually we converse in Dakota as that is the language of my wife's people. It is not acceptable for any man to speak to the woman of another without him present, and never is it allowed for a young woman of her age," nodding to Fawn," to speak to a man, unless she first has the permission of her father."

Jacques looked from Tate to Sean and then to his daughter, "I give my Reindeer Fawn my permission to speak with Sean, but no others." He nodded to Sean and his daughter, let a slight grin cross his face to break his stern mood, and looked back to Tate. "Among my people, I would have the right to take the lives of these men that have insulted my family. But, this time, I will not, if they apologize."

"Jacques, you are right. What these men have done is not acceptable in any culture. These are young men that have come from a different world than what we," motioning to himself and the others, "are used to, and haven't been taught the respect they need to learn. I don't know what it's going to take to make men out of these boys, but this is going to be a lesson they will have to learn. One way or the other, they will apologize, but I think I'm going to have to come up with some new ideas to make this lesson stick." He dropped his head, thought a moment, then looked up to Jacques, "Are your women very skilled with the bow?"

Jacques grinned as he saw the mischievous light sparkle in Tate's eyes, and nodded enthusiastically, "*Mais Oui!* Both of them can take a bird in flight with the first arrow!"

"Ha! That's great, now, here's what we'll do . . . " and he began to lay out his plan for the first lesson in wilderness manners.

CHAPTER EIGHTEEN
LESSON

Dusk stretched the vague shadows of the tall cottonwoods in parallel lines at a sharp angle to the riverbank. The eight Yale alumni were seated around the fire near the second wagon of the train while the four servants were busy with the usual cleanup. The men at the fire each held their coffee cups near as they shared their thoughts about the grand adventure, laughing at one another's experiences and thoughts of their journey. Five dark figures approached from beyond the circle of wagons, but the young men paid little attention.

As the shadowy figures stopped to observe, low voices told of the identities of the different men and where each was seated. The shadows dispersed, each approaching the ring of fire from different points, and when the mustachioed man charged into the circle, men shouted and jumped, spilling coffee and stumbling backwards. Jacques vaulted the edge of the fire and grasped the shirt front of the slender Malcolm whose wide eyes and stammering voice showed his alarm and fear.

The lunge of the Métis carried the two men away from the fire and to the nearby trees. Malcolm was back peddling and stumbling with only the grip of a mad father keeping him upright. His eyes were wide and mouth open as he stuttered in fear, with the only sound coming from his choked off throat one of gasping for air\ that sounded much like the squeal of a stuck pig. The treeline was only a few feet from the fire and Jacques pushed Malcolm back until he was pinned against a tall cottonwood, feet spread, and arms flung to the side as he fought for balance and footing.

"YOU!! You have insulted my woman and disgraced my daughter!" Jacques had his more than a foot-long Bowie knife at his side and lifted it. "For that you shall die!" he shouted, as the glint of light showed the razor-sharp knife held at the throat of the frightened young man.

Malcolm's eyes flared wider as he fought for air, kicking his feet until he realized he was held off the ground by this man.. He looked past the whiskered face and foul-smelling breath for any sign of help from his friends, but they stood, watching, showing fear and confusion on their faces. No one moved to help the youth who waved his hands and kicked his feet.

At about 5'8," Jacques was not a tall man and the perpetrator had at least four inches more height, but the Métis was broad with muscle that showed through the plaid patterned flannel shirt and wool britches. It demanded little effort for him to keep the youth suspended against the tree and Jacques snarled and spat to show to emphasize his rage..

"What'd I do? I didn't hurt anyone! What do you mean?!" stammered the terrified curly-haired blonde. He looked to the others, "Don't just stand there! Help me!" he demanded. "Get this crazy man . . ." but the press of the blade against his throat silenced him and he froze in place, feeling the trickle of blood course it's way down his neck. "Oh, oh, . . "

"It ees my right to kill you!" snarled Jacques, eyes pinching and lip curling in a snarl. "But I think I will take my time!"

A wave of Malcolm's hand made Jacques lessen the pressure just enough for Malcolm to speak, and the young man looked to Tate, "Help me, please!" he pleaded.

"Sorry son, like he said, it is his right to kill you. And after what you done, I can't say as I blame him!"

"What'd I do?" begged the horrified man.

"Well, you insulted his wife and daughter. Out here, a man doesn't speak to another man's wife, especially the way you did!"

"But, but, uh, they couldn't understand what we were saying!"

Jacques pushed with his meaty paw that gripped the front of the man's shirt and spat, "My family understands and speaks more languages than you!!"

Tate added, "That's right, those women speak, let me see," and he held out his opened hand to count on his fingers, "French, English, Dakota, Ojibwe, Cree, sign language, and more! But in their culture, they are not allowed to speak to any man unless the man of their lodge gives permission, and for any man to speak to them, that, my friend, is punishable by death. It is the ultimate disgrace. And when anyone speaks to any woman out here in the west, like the two of you did, most white men would kill you too!"

"But, but, that's not right! We didn't know!"

"Son, from what I've seen of you, you don't know anything about good manners or respect for anyone! You've looked down your nose at everybody here, thinking you were better than everyone! Now, it looks like you're gonna get your comeuppance! At the very least, it's gonna be a bit of a wilderness education about respect for all these others to learn!" he motioned toward the others with a wide swing of his arm.

A sudden commotion to the side parted the semi-circle of men as Erastus Throckmorton pushed his way through, but he wasn't coming to the aid of his friend. Behind him were Red Leaf and Reindeer Fawn, both holding bows with nocked arrows pointed at the man as he staggered toward his suspended friend. He had tried to flee when Jacques grabbed Malcolm, but the women were waiting, expecting just that.

Erastus looked at Tate and pleaded, "Please! You can't let them do this!"

"Why? Because they are not as good as you? Or is it because they are some of those 'savages' you looked down on?"

"There are laws! You can't just kill us! That's murder!" whined Malcolm.

The motion from the women pushed Erastus against the tree beside his friend, but he was held there by nothing but his fear and the threat of the women. He threatened, "The law will hunt you down for this!"

"Boys, I told all of you before," explained Tate, "The only law out here is what we make it. There are no courts, no judges, and thankfully no lawyers! The only thing that works here is to respect one another and their way of life. Now, the law of the Métis and other native peoples has been the law of their land for centuries and it works for them quite well." He looked at the others that stood watching, "What these fellas have done would result in a challenge to a duel back east, among whites, it would result in a hanging, and with the natives, it's all up to the man of the lodge. Right now, the lives of both these men are in his hands!"

"But, you can stop him!" declared Louis Reale, defiantly.

"Why should I? That pup," Tate motioned to Malcolm, "has been plotting to strike out at me for the last lesson he didn't learn, and he refuses to show respect to anyone, you included! But, I will say this, I'm sure that Jacques will give these boys a choice." He walked closer to Jacques and spoke to both him and the others, "Whadda ya' say, Jacques. Wanna give them a choice?"

Jacques looked to Tate, back to the one he held against the tree and then to the other nearby, and said, "*Oui!* I will give them a choice. They can let the women shoot them with ze bow an' arrow from a running horse, or," and he thought for a moment, "they can stand as a target and let the women shoot the arrows from back there," nodding his head beyond the fire. At that suggestion, Fawn loosed an arrow that caught the collar of Malcolm, pinning him to the tree. At the same time, Red Leaf sent her arrow to pin Erastus by the shirtsleeve just under his armpit.

Both men let out a gasp and looked to Tate for deliverance which did not come.

"Or, I can carve them up very slowly. First, I will cut off their ears," and with each description he moved the knife to touch each part, "then I will cut off the nose, then," and he dropped his eyes to the man's belt, "Wal, then . . . then I will scalp him, and if he still is not dead, I will feed his body to the buzzard." He brought his knife back to the man's throat, applied just enough pressure to bring a small trickle of blood.

"Oh, oh . . . oh, noooo," pleaded Malcolm as his bowels and bladder both released their contents.

Jacques stepped back so his boots would not be soiled, still leaning against Malcolm to hold him in place. He looked up at the red face, and with nose wrinkled in disgust, Jacques said, "You are not a man, you are a scared little boy!"

Jacques released his grip and moved back, looking carefully where he stepped. Malcolm still hung suspended by the arrow through his collar which he grabbed at, but stopped when Tate asked Jacques, "So, what do you choose?"

He looked at the two squirming specimens, and back at

Tate, then spoke loudly enough for all to hear, "If they will apologize to my women, they will live!"

Everyone looked to the two men, Erastus looked to Malcolm, and the one who caused all the problem, spat and answered, "I will not apologize to any savage!" The words had barely escaped his lips when another arrow whispered through the air and caught Malcolm's shirt under his right armpit. With the first arrow holding his collar on the left side, the second arrow successfully had him pinned to the tree, his feet still not touching the ground.

Malcolm sucked air when the second arrow struck, and he squealed again as he kicked and fought for freedom.

"You better apologize, young'un!" declared Tate.

"Never!" he retorted. And another arrow cut his right ear as it impaled itself into the bark. Before he could even squeal, another thunked into the cottonwood between his legs,very close to his crotch.

All eyes went to the second man, and two arrows hit the tree simultaneously, one on either side of the man's head, one bringing blood from an ear. Erastus immediately said, "I apologize! I apologize! I'll never disrespect any woman, ever!" he shouted, grabbing at his crotch, fearful of another arrow.

Malcolm scowled at his friend, glared at Tate and pinched his lips. Two arrows came from bowstrings that twanged in the silence and one shaft protruded from the upper arm of Malcolm and the second cut flesh in his opposite leg. The young man screamed, "No! No! No more! I'll apologize! I'm sorry! I won't ever do that again! I'm sorry!" As he spoke, his eyes filled with tears, but he could not move without adding to his pain. Blood was coming down his arm to drip from his fingers, and he looked down, and fell into unconsciousness.

Tate looked at the others, "Get him down, fellas. That shaft in his arm, you'll have to break it, and if you got some whiskey, pour it into the wound and bind him up real tight. He'll have something to remember 'bout all that, but at least he's alive, for now."

WITH THE BRIEF storm of the night and the incident with the two pilgrims, Tate chose to forego the buffalo hunt in favor of making time with the wagons. It was a somber bunch that took to the trail that morning, but a hard lesson had hopefully been learned by all. However, it wouldn't be until the wagons stopped at noon that John Richards discovered that both Malcolm and Erastus were missing from the train. When he questioned the others, he was told they left in the early morning and planned on meeting up with the east-bound stage out of Julesburg. The stage line was new to the west and had been founded to handle the needs of the many gold-seekers that were responding to the discovery of gold in Colorado. The sutler at Fort Kearny had told everyone about the stage line and the mail service it provided, and the two friends had been planning on leaving the train anyway. The incident of the night before just hastened their decision.

"Wal, I'd say that's too bad, but I never thought they'd make it anyway," declared Richards when he told Tate about the two leaving.

"When I heard him refer to his friends and everyone else as 'commoners' and that he thought he was better than the others, I knew then he would have some hard lessons to learn. Pity of it is, goin' back east to his 'cushy' life, he'll never learn those lessons, don't reckon. Shame. It's just mighty hard for some folks to swallow their pride and admit when they're wrong."

Sean had listened to the conversation and agreed with his pa, even though he didn't fully understand everything about what happened. He thought to himself, *Don't know why some folks gotta think themselves better'n others.* He looked down at the black wolf beside him, "Indy, that's why I'd rather sleep with wolves than spend time with some o' them men!"

CHAPTER NINETEEN
LANDMARKS

"PA SAID TO WATCH FOR TWO BIG ROCK FORMATIONS, BUT I never thought they'd be that big!" declared Sean, looking through his dad's brass telescope at the promontories in the distance. He rolled to his side, handed the scope to Fawn, "Take a look!"

It was the girl's first time to use the telescope and she was shocked at her first view. The big formations had been named Courthouse Rock and Jail Rock by earlier travelers on the Oregon Trail. Fawn leaned back, looked at the scope and over to a grinning Sean, and put it back to her eye again. "That is wonderful, I can see everything! Look, there's a doe and her fawn walking to the river!"

"Uh, I can't see it without the scope," answered Sean sheepishly. The past six days had been an exciting and enjoyable time for the two youngsters. They discovered their birthdays were only a month apart, with Sean being the oldest, and so many of their interests were similar as well. Fawn enjoyed reading as much as Sean, and they often spent the evenings by the fire, reading aloud to the others. Their current tome was *David Copperfield* by Charles Dickens, and Tate had found a copy of a poem he rather liked by Alfred Lord Tennyson, *"Charge of the Light Brigade"* and asked Sean to read it. The poem elicited much discussion, but all seemed to like it as read by Sean. Now, with six days riding together, the friendship between the two had grown considerably. Neither had a friend of the opposite sex before, but that didn't hinder their many explorations of the new territory. Both loved to ride and with Indy and Lobo always with them, except for this day, and laughter was a constant companion.

As Sean put the scope to his eye, he quickly spotted the doe and her offspring, and looked around the butte, but a sudden gasp caught the attention of Fawn, "What? What happened?"

Sean handed her the scope without speaking and watched as she lifted the long tube to her eye. "Oh! Those are Dakota! There are four of them!" she exclaimed as she watched the natives bending over the carcass of the fallen doe. "But the poor fawn! They killed it too!"

"Ummhumm. They might not o' seen the fawn till after they killed the doe. So, they killed it cuz it wouldn't survive anyway."

"Maybe, but still . . ." she replied as she continued watching.

"Is there just the four or are there more?" asked Sean, letting Fawn use the scope without interference.

"Looks like just the four, but they wouldn't be this far south without others. My mother is a Dakota, of the Santee, but these are the Lakota, maybe the Yankton. My mother said both Dakota and Lakota were together once long ago, but many left the lands to the north and moved west. That is one reason we were on this journey, to see some of these people that were once a part of our people."

"Well, me'n my family have made friends with many different native tribes, but never with the Sioux, or Lakota, as you call them. We just haven't been over here in this part of the country much." He rolled to his back and sat up, "Let's be gettin' back to the wagons, Pa'll wanna know 'bout them Lakota."

Sean waited as Fawn swung up on her mount, but as they turned to ride back, they were stopped with a barrier of five stern-faced warriors, all mounted and in a slight semi-circle blocking the trail. The memory of the recent display of cowardice by the weakling of the collegians gave Sean added resolve to show no weakness before these warriors. He raised his right hand, palm facing the band, and spoke, "A-ho!" He started to use sign language, but the voice of Fawn stopped him as she addressed the warriors in Dakota.

"I am Reindeer Fawn of the Santee Dakota, and this is Bear Chaser of the family of Saint, also known as Longbow. We are traveling with many wagons of the trader John Richards of Fort Bernard. This man has traded with the Sioux people and has been a friend to them. You should come with us to talk to the trader as he has many goods to share with your people."

"Ha!" declared the warrior at the front of the band, "I am Spotted Tail, war leader of the Brulé band of the Lakota! We will not go to the trader Richards, you will come with us!" At that growled command, two warriors gigged their horses forward to come alongside both Sean and Fawn, snatching the reins of their mounts and pressing spear tips to their midriffs. Sean slowly lifted his hands as did Fawn, but Sean casually turned up the collar of his tunic to hide the knife hanging between his shoulder blades beneath the buckskin.. He also had to force himself not to reach under the tail of his tunic for his Colt Navy revolver, as he knew he was still at a considerable disadvantage. Maybe he could get one, perhaps two, but they would eventually overwhelm him and then what would happen to Fawn?

One warrior grabbed at the protruding stock of the Hawken in Sean's scabbard, pulled it free and lifted it overhead with a war-whoop. Although Sean and Fawn had been using their bows, Sean still carried his rifle and shook his head as the broad-nosed warrior shouted again at his discovery of the weapon. He looked to Fawn and was proud of her as she sat ramrod straight, head lifted, a proud look on her face as if daring their captors to harm them. She showed no concern and glanced to Sean, showing a slight smirk of confidence and a bit of a nod to show her friend she was not afraid.

The warriors used their mounts to bump the rears of Sean and Fawn's horses to prod them forward. With the leader, Spotted Tail, and one other warrior, apparently his second-in-command, in the lead, the other warriors followed behind the captives as the group dropped from the timber covered knoll toward a brush filled draw. Sean looked around, scanning the overall area, and realized they would be out of sight of his pa and Jacques, but he wasn't concerned knowing his pa had the reputation of being able to track an eagle on the wing, and he would find them.

TATE LEANED FORWARD on his pommel, looking at the tracks, turned to Jacques, "Looks like our young'uns have been taken, probably by some Sioux!"

"*Oui!*" answered Jacques. He was on one knee, examining the tracks closely and added, "Five, maybe six, they met there," pointing to the narrow break in the trees, "and went down toward that ravine. They were moving at a walk, no hurry."

"Either they haven't spotted the wagons, or they just don't care.. If they knew about the wagons, and they're not concerned, that would mean they're with a large encampment nearby."

"*Oui*," agreed Jacques, standing to remount.

"The wagons need to know, but we also need to follow an' see where they went," declared Tate, nodding his head in the direction of the tracks.

"*Mais Oui,* but I do not care about the wagons as much as I care about my daughter!" exclaimed the Métis.

"Look, we just hung that deer for 'em back yonder an' I've got Maggie's writing paraphernalia, so let's just put a note on that carcass an' Richards'll find it and know where we went."

Jacques nodded his head and let a grin cross his face, then frowned as he looked to Tate. "You make the note, I will follow them," nodding toward the tracks, "and you will follow me!"

Tate could tell by the look of determination on the face of the hard-headed Métis there would be no arguing with him, so he just nodded and reined Shady around, kicked him up to a canter, and headed for the hanging deer carcass. He had just finished his note and was standing in his stirrups to tuck the paper under the braided rawhide when he glanced to the road and saw the wagons approaching. Although he had no intention of waiting for them to arrive, he saw Richards had kicked his horse to a trot and was headed in his direction. Tate dropped into his saddle to wait for his friend and to explain what happened.

"So ya' see, John, me'n Jacques need to go get our kids!" summarized Tate, "and you need to see to your wagons an' such."

"Yeah, an' I ain't surprised none. After that run-in at the hands of that shavetail West Point Lieutenant Grattan a couple years back, them Sioux have turned their backs on that treaty they signed in '51 at Laramie and pretty much done whatever they wanted. They figger they showed the army they ain't scared of 'em and the army ain't done much o' nuthin' 'bout it, neither.

"Mebbe you oughta take a few with you, like maybe one o' them college kids and one o' my men that might help out, you know, like ol' Bucky Roberts, he's a pretty good hand in a fight."

Tate gave the idea quick consideration, "Mebbe, but that also gave me another idea. You get Bucky an' maybe that young'un name o' Patrick, he can hit what he aims at, an' I'll get my other rifle outta the wagon. Have 'em ready to go quick as you can!" Before Richards could reply, Tate had Shady on a run toward the last wagon where his gear had been stowed. He grasped the other Spencer rifle, jammed his pockets full of cartridges, took his longbow and quiver, and stepped back aboard Shady to meet John and the others at the head of the wagons.

"We're going after some Indians?" asked Patrick incredulously as Tate reined up beside the two men. He looked to Tate expectantly but with veiled expression.

"That's right, and if you don't think you're up to it, you don't have to come along."

Patrick looked to Bucky, back at Tate and with a grin, "Oh, I think I'm up to it. Let's go!"

TATE DUG heels into the ribs of Shady and took him to a canter. Bucky and Patrick kicked at their mounts to catch up with the anxious Tate and the three were soon on the trail left by the fleeing captors. The tracks were easily followed with no sign of anyone trying to mask them and the prints of Jacques' mount held to the side, making the task that much easier. Tate kept Shady at a ground-eating canter, never taking his eyes from the sign that pointed the way to his son. Suddenly, the tracks of Jacques mount turned and Tate reined up, confused. He leaned down for a closer look, lifted his eyes in the direction they pointed, back at the tracks and turned to the others. "Jacques has taken to that hill yonder, reckon he's got some idea where them Sioux are headed. Let's follow, if he goes astray, we can always pick up the trail farther on."

Tate didn't wait for a response from his two companions, as Shady kicked dirt as he leapt to the trail that pointed up the slight knoll. Tate thought this was the first rise that was bigger than an ant hill since they left Fort Kearny, and he believed Jacques wanted to have a promontory to spot the captors and perhaps locate their destination.

With Shady humping his back and digging with all four hooves, they soon neared the pinnacle of the sage covered hill. As he suspected, Tate spotted Jacques' horse tethered to a scrub oak and the man was belly down at the crest of the mound. Tate motioned to the others to stop where they were, and he stepped down to hand the reins of his mount to Patrick. Tate hunkered down, made his way near Jacques, then crawled to the side of his friend. Jacques had a spyglass to his eye and spoke to Tate without moving, "I see the band, yonder in a gully beyond that cut."

Tate shaded his eyes to look where Jacques pointed, and could barely make out movement of black in the distance. "Can you see our young'uns?"

"*Oui*, I think they are alright. There is water in the bottom there, but I don't think they are stopping to camp. Mebbe just to rest the animals. There are others that have joined them, now there are at least ten, and there may be more. This is a hunting party, but they have not taken much game."

"Ya think we can catch 'em 'fore dark?"

"*Mais Oui!* We can take this way," he pointed to a break in the hills that opened to a narrow valley, "and if we move quickly, we can come out ahead of them!"

"Then let's get a move on!" declared Tate as he crabbed his way back from the crest of the hill. He was followed by Jacques and the men were soon mounted and starting down the far slope. Tate muttered a silent prayer as they hit the flats and took to an all-out run. Their route was obscured from the view of the Sioux and they were not concerned about a dust plume or anything that would give them away, believing the Sioux to be unconcerned about any pursuers.

From the hilltop, Jacques and Tate had sighted a long ridge that appeared as a spine with many finger ridges on both sides. They chose the southeast side where the wide gully was bottomed with a dry and sandy creek bed. Believing it to be low enough to keep them hidden from the hunting party as long as they stayed in the creek bottom with ample greenery and water on the opposite side of the long ridge. They did not spare their horses, anxious to overtake the captors.

Within the hour they approached the end of the ridge and they slowed as Tate motioned. He had said he would take to the ridge for a look see. The others dismounted, giving their horses a breather, Jacques holding the leads of both his big bay and Tate's grulla. Tate scampered up the slope, bellied down into the sandy soil and peered over the crest to see the hunting party nearing the head of the ravine and just over three hundred yards away. He crabbed his way back, and with long strides and heels digging into the soil, he descended the slope.

He was breathing heavy as he went to Shady and grabbed

his longbow from its sheath under the fender of his left stirrup. He snatched the quiver from behind the cantle and
looked to Jacques, "I've got to stop them 'fore they get to the
end of that ravine. There's a bit of a canyon they could duck
into an' we might lose 'em. Sit tight, I'll be right back."

CHAPTER TWENTY
PURSUIT

THE LONGBOW HAD ALWAYS BEEN TATE'S WEAPON OF CHOICE. From the time he and his father studied the tactics and weapons of medieval warfare and the history of their forefathers among the English and Welsh, both had been fascinated with the English longbow. His father described it as the most powerful weapon of its day when they resolved to build and master the weapon. When Tate left Missouri after the death of his mother and father, he had the best and last of the many yew longbows they built together. It had taken several years for the young man to master the bow, but when he walked away from his father's graveside, he had become a journeyman at both making and using the weapon.

On his trek to the west and his early years in the mountains, his skill with the longbow had earned him the respect of many of the native peoples. Its power, range, and his accuracy earned him the name Longbow, bestowed upon him by the chief of the Kiowa, Dohäsan. A moniker that had proven his worth and respect among the many tribes of the mountains and the plains. But he had never encountered the Sioux, and that was soon to change.

Tate found a large flat shoulder just below the pinnacle of the ridge and he took his position. With the hunting party now moving from his left to the right, he would be in position to make the shot he wanted. The distance of just over two hundred yards was nothing for the man, having made many shots beyond three hundred yards. He stepped into the bow, bringing the thirty-inch arrow to its full draw and with a deep breath, letting it out just a mite, and sighting down the shaft, he let the feathered missile fly.

WHEN THE ARROW whispered past the noses of the leader's horses, the animals shied back, lifting their heads and prancing backwards. The riders were startled and when Spotted Tail saw the quivering shaft protruding from the soil of the bank beside the trail, his eyes grew large as he shouted, "Down, an attack! From there!" he pointed to the slight hillside that rose from the creek bottom as he slipped to the far side of his mount, sheltering himself behind the skittish animal. The other warriors jumped from their horses and sought cover among the willows and buffaloberry bushes by the creek. The horses, unsure of what was happening, turned from the trail and followed their riders into the creek bottom.

Sean and Fawn sat in their saddles, their wrists having been tied to the horns, and Sean started laughing. "One arrow and you're all running! What kind of warriors are you?" and laughed as he motioned for Fawn to translate his words into the language of the Lakota.

Spotted Tail heard the words and looked at the white man, "Who is this that sends an arrow at Spotted Tail? He must not be much of a warrior, I do not see him. Does he hide because he cannot hit his mark?" The chief had regained his braggadocio as he stepped from behind his horse, walking toward Sean.

When Fawn told Sean the words of the chief, Sean responded, "He does not hide." Sean motioned with his chin toward the far ridge where his father stood boldly on the skyline. "And he could send an arrow through your heart at any time. He is Longbow, known and respected by the Kiowa, the Pawnee, the Comanche, Apache, Ute, Arapaho, and feared by the Blackfeet! He is my father and he is not happy you have taken us!"

Spotted Tail looked at the man on the skyline, and back at Sean, "Ha! No man can send an arrow that far! There must be others nearby!"

"Oh, there are others alright, but he's the only one with a longbow. The others have shoots far rifles that have many bullets. They can shoot faster than your warriors can send their arrows." Sean watched the reaction of the skeptical chief and continued, "But, I tell you what. You put a blanket on that bush yonder, and I'll have my father put an arrow in the middle of it, just to show you what a great warrior he is."

"Ha! It cannot be done!" declared the chief but motioned for one of his warriors to do as bidden. Once the blanket was spread on the bush, Sean was surprised when Spotted Tail cut the bonds at his wrist and jerked him from his saddle. With another man holding one arm while the chief held the other, they dragged Sean to the blanket, stood him on his feet and motioned for him to stay by the blanket. "Now, you have him," pointing to the man on the skyline, "put an arrow in the blanket beside you!"

Sean chuckled, and waved his hand at his pa, motioned to the blanket, and stood quietly beside the spread cover. As many warriors and the chief watched the figure on the ridge, Tate nocked another arrow, stepped into the bow bringing it to full draw, and quickly released themissle. The onlookers heard rather than saw the passing arrow, but their heads quickly turned to see the impaled shaft with only the feather fletching protruding from the quivering blanket. A collective gasp came from the group and many turned back to see the archer on the ridge, still standing and waiting. But they could also see he held another nocked arrow in his bowstring.

Spotted Tail extracted it from the blanket and was surprised to see the length of the shaft. The average arrow of a plains Indian was about twenty- four inches, while the arrow he held in his hand was just over thirty inches long. He lifted his eyes to the man on the ridge and looked back to Sean. "I would have this bow!"

"Wouldn't do you any good. Several have tried, but no one has been able to pull that bow to a full draw except my Pa."

Spotted Tail narrowed his eyes as he looked at Sean, then looked toward the man on the ridge. "If I cannot draw the bow, you can go free."

"And Reindeer Fawn?"

"No, I will keep her for my woman. My first wife would have a helper and she is young."

"No deal. I suggest you let us go now, or you will lose many men in the fight to come. Those that are with my pa will rain down bullets like you ain't never seen!" declared Sean, hoping his father did have some help and the Spencer repeating rifles.

"No!" declared Spotted Tail. When that was said, Sean lifted his hands together as if they were tied and dropped to his knees. His father understood and in less that a quick breath, and arrow pierced the chest of the man that always stood at the side of Spotted Tail, and the man staggered back from the blow, looked down at the fletching, and gave a frightened expression as he dropped to his knees, then fell forward on his face.

For just an instant, Spotted Tail stared at the body of his

friend then looked back to the ridge to see Tate disappear behind the crest, but another arrow had already found its mark in the neck of the warrior standing beside Spotted Tail. The chief quickly pulled his knife, pushed Sean toward his horse and jumped for his own mount as he shouted orders to his men to take to their horses.

The men were no sooner mounting than gunfire erupted from both sides of the ravine. The smattering of shots came quickly and accurately, and warriors began falling . Sean hollered to Fawn, "Let's go!" and dug his heels into Dusty's ribs causing the big Appaloosa to lunge forward. He glanced back to see Fawn was close behind and both leaned low on the necks of their horses as they thundered away from the melee.

Jacques and Patrick, at Tate's suggestion, had taken to the far side of the ravine while Bucky had stayed on the same side as Tate, but the big teamster had worked down close to the ravine when the Sioux were focused on Tate. When the chief had shouted for the others to follow him as he started to leave, Jacques opened the battle with his Hawken, prompting both Patrick and Bucky to cut loose with the Spencers. Once Tate dropped the bow, he brought up his big Sharps and began methodically picking off his targets.

While Patrick and Bucky kept the confusion and fear going with their repeated firing of the Spencers, their aim wasn't near as good as Tate with his Sharps and Jacques who was closer in with his Hawken. Both men seldom missed, and the numbers of the Sioux rapidly diminished until Tate shouted, and the firing ceased. Several horses had taken stray bullets and some lay wounded and struggling, a few warriors still lived though injured, and only two had yet to feel the sting of lead, but they cowered behind the cover of the creek-side brush.

Tate worked his way closer but refused to take a risk of

showing himself until he was certain of his steps and safety. He shouted to Jacques, "What'chu think Jacques?"

"There are two still living, wait." He hollered to the hidden warriors in Dakota, "Come out from the bushes, we will not shoot you, if you drop your weapons and raise your hands. Now!" he demanded. For a moment nothing moved, but then the two warriors, both very young, pushed aside the brush and stood, hands raised. Jacques hollered to Tate, "They are two young boys, no one else lives!"

Tate and Jacques approached with Patrick and Bucky following, all holding their rifles at the ready. Jacques told the two youngsters, who looked to be about twelve or at most thirteen, to sit on the grass and wait. Tate walked from warrior to warrior, and when he came to Spotted Tail, he saw the man still lived, but had a bad wound to his upper right chest. Tate motioned for Jacques to come near and spoke to the man lying on the grass, "You are the leader?" he asked.

Jacques translated, and the man nodded, struggled to speak, "I am Spotted Tail, war chief of the Brulé Sioux."

"Unless I miss my guess, Spotted Tail, I believe my son, Bear Chaser, told you this didn't have to happen. Am I right?"

"Yes, but I wanted the young woman for my lodge. I did not believe him."

"If we patch you up, ya' think you can ride? You've got a couple youngsters here that can help you."

"You would let me go?" asked a bewildered Spotted Tail.

"I have my son, and Jacques has his daughter," he nodded with his head to indicate the returning riders. "You do not need to die. Maybe you learned something here today," stated Tate as he waved his hand toward the bodies. The sudden report of a rifle startled the group, but it was just Bucky putting a wounded horse out of his misery. "I don't know if you'll live, that's a pretty nasty hole you've got there, but we can patch you up and you can try to make it back to your village."

"I will go." He lifted his eyes to Tate, "You are Longbow?"

"Yup, that's me." He pointed to the bow that was now at his back beneath the quiver and extended over his left shoulder and below his right hip. It measured just over six feet and when unstrung, looked like a long pole, but it was indeed a deadly weapon.

Tate saw the chief's eyes look to the bow, and the man asked, "Could I have drawn the bow?"

"Well, one thing's for sure, you couldn't now. But many have tried, and none have been able to bring it to a full draw. It's because this bow requires a lot of strength, and a lot of experience. It took me several years to master."

The chief nodded his head as he struggled to his feet, but as he stood, he stumbled when he saw the big grey wolf standing beside the white man. He lifted his eyes to Tate and back to the wolf, then he sat on a big flat boulder and waited as Jacques tended his wound. Once the Métis finished, he introduced himself, "I am Jacques Bottineau of the Métis people from far to the north. My woman is a Santee Dakota and we have come to meet the people that were once with her people. We will be with this man, and the buffalo hunters northwest of Fort Laramie. If you come, we will share our meat with you and your people."

Spotted Tail nodded his head, stood, looked to Tate and with the aid of the two young warriors, mounted his horse. The two joined him and with nothing more than a nod, Spotted Tail rode into the notch between the hills and was soon out of sight.

Jacques looked to Tate and said, "What you did! I have never seen such a thing!" He looked around and back to Tate, "What about all this?" motioning to the scattered bodies. Bucky and Patrick had joined them, also looking to Tate for an answer. Tate had noted that neither man had been very talkative, and he had seen Patrick empty his stomach after he saw the bodies of the many warriors.

Tate answered, "He'll send others back for them. I don't think their village is too far, but he has been shamed and with the two young'uns to tell the truth, I'm sure our wagons won't be bothered, so, how 'bout we get back to them?"

"*Mais Oui!* My woman will be worried about her little one!" declared Jacques as he looked up to his smiling Reindeer Fawn. He reached for her hand and she bent to give her father a hug, leaning down from atop her saddle.

Sean watched, grinning, and relieved they were with their fathers and not hanging spread-eagled in some Sioux camp. He breathed deep and nudged Dusty forward to ride beside Fawn once again. She smiled, reached out her hand to clasp his and they rode side by side, each one trying to forget what had just happened and how close they came to being slaves in the camp of the Brulé Sioux.

SEAN AND TATE SAT ON THE FLAT BLUFF OVERLOOKING THE
North Platte. Beyond the river rose the two-headed bluff
that was the central landmark for the territory. While the
Oregon Trail and its deep wagon ruts stayed on the south
side of the river, the trader Richards' wagons were following
what had become known as the Mormon Trail on the north
side. The trail below the bluff followed the meandering
course of the river and avoided the buttes bluffs and hills
that bordered the northern plains. With so many of the
emigrating Mormons utilizing the handcarts made available
by decree from their leaders, their choice of trail demanded
the more level, though circuitous route that avoided the ups
and downs that marked these western plains.

Sean stood in his stirrups and pointed to the south west,
"Look Pa, you can still see that Chimney Rock from here.
How far ya' reckon that is?" Sean had been fascinated with
the unusual landmarks in this country. The first were the
two formations seen by Fawn and him before their set-to
with the Sioux, then the unusual Chimney Rock held him
spellbound as he stared at the towering obelisk. He told his

pa it made him think that was where the devil was buried, and he had stabbed his accusing finger toward heaven as his last act. Then the rimrock formations of the big bluffs just across the river from where they now sat, stirred his imagination once again. "An' that yonder, that could be where God buried that giant, what's-his-name, the one David knocked out with his sling."

"You must be thinkin' 'bout Goliath! Well, I s'pose it's just as likely that could be where Goliath is, if you wanna believe the Chimney Rock is the devil's pointer! But, I'm purty sure Goliath was a long way from here when David felled him, and as I recall, the devil ain't been buried yet."

"So, how far?" asked Sean, pointing with his chin to the distant pillar that seemed to hold up the blue sky.

"Oh, as the crow flies, probably near onto twenty miles."

"If we weren't up on this knob, we couldn't make it out. Not like when we're in the mountains. But it sure is good to see somethin' that resembles a mountain, even it they ain't much more'n anthills. I'm almighty tired of this flat land!"

"I know what'chu mean son, I've been hankerin' to see the mountains myself. But, for now, let's get down there nearer the river, we might get us a couple deer 'fore the wagons catch up."

"I'm ready!" responded the lad. Since their run-in with the Sioux, Jacques had stayed back with his women folk and the only time Sean got to see Fawn was when they camped for the night. He and his pa most often took their supper with the family, and Sean had to tell Fawn all about the scout for the day. Although it had only been three days since the Siouxincident, there would be at least two more days before they gained Fort Bernard and Jacques had made himself clear that Fawn would stay with her mother until then.

When they jumped the deer at the edge of the river, both Sean and Tate scored a hit with their bows. They had chosen to travel as quietly as possible, not wanting a repeat of the episode with the Sioux and the easiest way was to use their bows for the meat-getting. They had barely finished dressing out the deer when they heard the approach of the wagons and they stood and stretched to wave the train into the camp area.

As the wagons made their semi-circle, two deep, against the slight bluff, Tate and Sean had thrown the carcasses over their saddles and started back, just in time to see three mounted visitors approaching the still mounted John Richards. With no hostility being shown, Tate and son took the meat to the main cookfire, dropped it for Cooky and reserved two backstrap loins for their own use. As they neared the off-set camp of Jacques, Tate noticed Richards motioning for him to come. He handed Sean the reins of Shady, so he could stake the horses out on the grass, and nodded his approval when Sean asked if he could stay with the family.

"TATE, this is Jim Baker and his wife, Flying Fox, and this other varmint is John Johnson," stated John Richards, grinning as he introduced the visitors. They had already dismounted and had pulled a log toward the fire for their seat.

Tate walked close, extended his hand to Baker, "Howdy Jim. Been a while."

"It certainly has, Tate. How's the family?"

Richards   interjected   incredulously,   "You   know each other?"

Tate grinned, "Oh yeah, this rascal almost got me killed a couple years back." He looked back to the visitor, "To answer your question, family's fine. Just comin' back from takin' my wife and daughter to St. Louis so they could tend to the girl's education, but my son is with me." He nodded back toward the small camp of Jacques. He stepped towards Johnson, extended his hand, "Don't believe I've met you b'fore John."

Baker laughed, "It's a good thing. Some folks call him 'Liver-Eatin' Johnson and it ain't too safe to be 'round him!"

Johnson picked up a small stick and threw it at his friend, laughing. "You ain't got nuthin' to worry 'bout, I don't think even a starvin' grizz would eat your rotten liver!"

"Coffee, Tate?" offered Richards, extending the pot and a cup.

Tate nodded, took a seat on the opposite side of the fire on another log and sipped his brew. He looked to Richards with a question on his face and John began, "Baker here's been scoutin' for General Harney outta Laramie, an' he says both the Cheyenne and the Sioux are gettin' a little restless. There's been some attacks on a few wagon trains earlier in the summer, nothin' in the last month though."

Tate looked to Baker, "Not scoutin' anymore?"

"No, no, we're headin' down to Colorado, course we're takin' the long way, but I figger with all them idjits goin' after gold, I might set up a tradin' post or sumpin' to supply 'em and let them find the gold then I'll take it from 'em by sellin' 'em muh stuff!" Baker's beady eyes showed a touch of humor as he wiped the coffee from his well-trimmed whiskers. His high cheekbones and narrow hatchet face bore testimony of the many hard winters spent in the mountains, and his lean frame stretched his long legs toward the fire. His well-padded woman sat close beside him and kept her hand tucked in the crook of his elbow, but her eyes were always downcast.

"Well, I reckon John here has told you what we have in store with this college kid brigade we got saddled with, so, you got any advice for us?" asked Tate, respectful of the man's many years in the mountains. He knew Jim spoke Arapaho,

Shoshone, and several other languages of the natives and had spent many winters with different bands, giving him an understanding and knowledge that bore mining.

"The best advice I can give you is for you an' all them chillen' to turn 'round and go back to St. Louie. But if'n that ain't happenin', then, keep a sharp eye out, watch your back, and don't trust any o' them Sioux or Cheyenne," spat the mountain man, emptying his coffee cup and tossing the dregs behind him.

"You think Harney will object to us goin' north after some buffalo?"

"Ha! I tell you what, there seems to be a growin' idee among them politicians an' west-pointers that the only way to tame these Injuns is to kill all the buffalo! Can you imagine such foolishness? All they're gonna do is get them Sioux an' Cheyenne, an' prob'ly a bunch o' others all fired up and then they'll have their hands full. An' what I hear comin' outta the east, I'm thinkin' there's gonna be war o'er this slavery issue and then what're they gonna do? "

"After what we saw in the city an' on the way out here, I'm beginnin' to think you might be right. What with the election comin' up next year an' Douglas an' Lincoln goin' at it, an' all this statehood and slavery fightin', I don't see how they're gonna stop it, 'cept goin' to war," stated Richards, poking at the fire.

"Is that what Harney thinks? I mean 'bout killin' the buffalo?" asked Tate, somewhat subdued. He had heard it said before when he was in St. Louis, but he couldn't believe people could think that killing the most prolific animal on the plains could stop an Indian war. After all, the buffalo was the main source of sustenance for the native peoples and they would zealously defend their land and their way of life. With buffalo providing meat, tools, hides for lodges, and fur for blankets and robes, most believed they could not survive without the beasts..

"When I was talkin' to him just th' other day, tellin' him I was leavin', I asked him about it. He told me that he keeps hearing it from those higher up in the command. With some of the tribes on the reservation, the only time they leave is to go on a buffalo hunt, their thinkin' is that without the buffalo, the Indians would be easier to control. They would be dependent on the white man's beef and would behave themselves. And you and I both know that kind of thinking is comin' from people that have never even seen an Indian or a buffalo, much less understands them. That's what happens when you get a bunch o' ninnies in suits an' they get all that power, it plumb goes to their empty head and they think they're smarter us plain folks!" declared Baker, spitting a gob of tobacco into the flames, then wiping the drool from his chin whiskers with his sleeve.

All the men shook their heads in consternation at the tide of things coming from the east. They sat silent for a short while, staring into the fire and pondering the demise of the way of life as they knew it.. Tate looked to the older man, "Any special area we oughta avoid when we go after these buffalo?"

"If'n I was you, I'd not go too far north. You know them ridges up above the North Platte, where the river turns back to the west? Well, I'd say you'd prob'ly find all the buffler you need up in that country, without getttin' too close to the Cheyenne or too far east into the Sioux stompin' grounds. But the farther you get from Fort Laramie, the more you're likely to run into ol' Red Cloud an' his Ogalala or Swift Bear an' some o' them Brulé."

Tate slowly lifted his head, deep in thought as he pictured the country spoken of, then looked to Baker, "Thanks Jim, sounds like good advice. You sure you don't wanna come along an' help me wean these bottle babies?"

He laughed, stubbed his toe in the dirt, "Naw, young'un, I had my share o' fightin' an' such, Flyin' Fox here's got me thinkin' peaceable like."

Tate stood, shook hands with the men, and said, "Well, you old-timers take care now, y'hear?"

Everyone laughed as Tate left the fire and started back to the camp of Jacques and family. He shook his head at what might be in store for him and his charges, more than what he bargained for, he opined. But that worry could keep for another day, now was the time to enjoy friends and family and good food. And, maybe a good night's rest, providing they were safe enough where they were and there weren't any Brulé looking for revenge.

CHAPTER TWENTY-TWO
FORT BERNARD

THE TRADING POST WAS CROWDED WITH THE MANY PILGRIMS from the wagon train that arrived the day before. With over twenty wagons, there was an abundance of travelers wanting to stock up in this last post before Fort Bridger. They had been told that Bridger wasn't as well supplied, and everyone was loading up before the long journey across the plains before reaching South Pass.

Tate and Sean pitched in to get the freighters unloaded and a few of the collegians had joined in with the effort. Tate had explained they would spend a day or two resting the animals before starting on this last leg of their grand adventure.

"So, Tate, do you think we'll get to the buffalo soon?" asked Patrick, his arms full of bundles for the post.

"We could run into 'em any day now. All this country is buffalo ground. Ya' see, Patrick, the herds migrate up from the south when spring comes, and they kinda mosey on toward the mountains till the cold weather threatens. Now, some of 'em hang around anyway, but the bigger part of the herds go back south. Since we're in mid-summer, we should find a herd or two 'fore too many days."

"Are they really that hard to bring down, like some folks say?" joined in Justis, who was also carrying bundles into the back storerooms of the trading post, although his load wasn't like what the others carried, but at least he was willing to help.

Tate had dropped his burden and leaned back against the stack of bundles, pushed his hat back, and looked at the two eager hunters. "Buffalo are almighty tough animals. A big bull can weigh over a ton and most cows top a thousand pounds. Their skull is so hard, at least the bull's, that it's a waste of lead to try a headshot. And their hide is thicker'n any other animal I know. Then when they're on the run, they're deceptively fast and it's easy to not get a kill shot. They can take a few bullets an' keep on goin' with you never knowin' you hit 'em. Then if one of 'em starts to charge you, there won't be any trees you can climb and you sure can't outrun 'em an' tryin' to shoot 'em in that thick skull, why, . . . " he shook his head, trying to keep from grinning at the greenhorns.

As Tate started for the doorway, Patrick and Justis looked at one another. "I think this is going to be a little more exciting than we figured, don't you?" remarked Patrick.

"I think you're right. But when we saw those buffalo back on the trail, they just looked like big cows to me," answered Justis as the two followed after Tate.

"But Tate said those were just a few stragglers. I guess it's different when there's a big herd."

It was early morning of the third day at Fort Bernard when the buffalo brigade pulled away from the trading post. Two of the covered wagons held all the personal gear, and the two big empty freighters, each pulled by a four-up of mules, rattled and squeaked as they followed the smaller wagons. Tate, Sean, Jacques and his family, all rode in the lead, with several of the collegians mounted and following. Bucky, the leader of the teamsters, cracked a whip over the mules of the first freighter, and the train of four wagons was followed by Festus Biddle and his son driving the extra stock.

They stayed to the well-traveled road toward Fort John, or Laramie as it was most often called. It would be a short jaunt to the bigger fort, just eight miles, but they planned on nooning there and giving Tate the opportunity to check in with the commandant.

Since the army had taken over the fort in '49, buying it from the American Fur Company, most of the trading and re-supplying was done at Fort Bernard. But the continual tide of settlers traveling the Oregon Trail necessitated the military provide some protection from the Indians and the Regiment of Mounted Rifles began the army's work at the fort. Now it was commanded by General William S. Harney of the Battle of Ash Hollow fame and several different units had been posted there.

As Tate was ushered into the General's office, the man barely glanced up from his paperwork but waved for him to be seated. The orderly retreated, closing the door behind him and at the sound, the General looked up. He looked back down at the paper before him and back to Tate. "Tate Saint, say, aren't you the one that did a little scouting with Baker a while back? Back when we had that trouble with them Crow renegades?"

Tate was surprised the man remembered. He had never met the General and his scouting was done with Jim Baker, with no direct contact with the soldiers. Tate grinned, "Yessir, I helped Jim out a little."

"A little? Why, the way I remember it, you practically

single-handedly stopped an all-out war with the Crow. That renegade, what's his name?"

"Bad Heart Bear," answered Tate, recalling the renegade's kidnapping of his wife and the subsequent chase.

"Well, from the way Baker told it, I guess you done him in, that right?"

"Ummhumm, that's right. Now General, . . . " Tate started but was interrupted.

"Oh yes, yes. You're guiding a bunch of buffalo hunters, that right? Well, I'm mighty glad to see more buffalo hunters. I'm beginning to agree with those higher-ups that believe if we were to eradicate the buffalo, we would have better control of the Indians!"

"Do you really believe that General? I mean, without them, what will the natives eat? Everything about their way of life is connected with the buffalo."

"That may be, but I for one am almighty tired of having to chase after a bunch of renegades just to get them back on the reservation. I've heard it said, with every dead buffalo there's an Indian gone! So, we welcome the hunters and encourage them to help us rid the plains of Indians!" he smacked the butt of his fist to the desktop to emphasize his point.

"I'm right sorry to hear you say that General, but I guess I'm a part of it since I'm taking this bunch into buffalo country."

"Well, give your buffalo brigade my welcome and support. I believe we'll be seeing many more hunters soon."

"Well, I wouldn't exactly call them buffalo hunters, at least not yet. They're more a bunch of city slickers out here on what they're calling a grand adventure. Really, they're a bunch of young men from prominent families that need to do some growin' up."

"Prominent families? Like who, for instance?"

"Well, I don't know everything about all of 'em, but, let me see. Their leader, Patrick, is a nephew of Andrew Carnegie. One fella is some kind of back-door relation to John Breckenridge," but before he could continue, the General interrupted again.

"Breckenridge? You mean the vice-president?"

"Ummhumm." Tate paused, then continued, "One is a brother-in-law to the Vanderbilts, and another one is connected with the Pennsylvania Railroad and is supposed to be scouting the country for a passage."

"Humm, well, maybe I should meet these youngsters." He stood, motioned for Tate to lead the way out of the office and grinned all the way. It was evident the man was thinking of making connections, though limited of course, with the young men and perhaps extending that to the families.

Once all the introductions had been made, the General made a show of interest as he spoke with the young men and their grand adventure. As the conversation waned, he turned to Tate, "I'm going to send a patrol out with you, just a show of force, actually, but it won't hurt for any of the Sioux and Cheyenne to show you're under the protection of the army."

"Well, General, since you said there hadn't been any problems with the natives, maybe that won't be necessary. But we appreciate it, anyway."

"Nonsense, no problem at all. These young men need to know we will do our utmost to provide all the protection they need." He nodded toward the group before turning back to Tate. "Besides, my troops need to stay sharp and a little patrol will help."

"Alright, General, if you insist. I'm gonna gather up a bunch o' letters these young men want to send back home, and then we'll be ready to pull out."

The General nodded, spun on his heel and retreated to his office. Tate had earlier told the men this would be their last chance to have any mail go out and suggested they write to their families. The gathered letters were put together with the one from Tate to Maggie and delivered to the post Sutler who also served as the Mail Officer. A short while later, everyone watched as a double line of twenty-four cavalry-men, led by Major Albemarle Cady, came through the gate and with bright swallow-tailed guidons and flags streaming in the wind. They were an impressive sight, and the collegian would-be hunters were thrilled.

Once away from the fort, one of the soldiers, a top sergeant O'Rourke, directed Tate, "The major would like to see you!"

Tate looked at the gruff sergeant and nodded his head. The man reined around and led Tate back to the head of the column of cavalry, saluted the major and motioned for Tate to ride beside the man.

The major looked at Tate as he would an underling and asked, "Your name Saint?"

"That's right," casually and intentionally drawled Tate, glancing sideways at the popinjay.

"Then perhaps you can tell me what this is all about. I'll have you know it is highly unusual and unorthodox to be sent out to accompany a bunch of buffalo hunters!"

Tate chuckled, "I think your commandant is doing this more to curry favor than to helphunters. These are not buffalo hunters like you might think. These are young men from influential families out on a grand adventure."

The major reined up, holding his hand high to stop the column, and looked at Tate, "Influential families?"

"Ummhumm."

"Why that old goat! No wonder. He'd do anything to try to gain some influence or connection with anyone in power. He's so anxious to get back east, I'm surprised he hasn't quit the army and left. That explains everything." He looked at Tate, "Well, we won't be with you long. We're supposed to be back at the post before full dark, so, we'll be leaving you soon." He reached into his pocket and extracted a card, handing it to Tate. "If I can ever be of service to you or your charges," nodding toward the wagons, "just send word. I don't think you'll have any trouble on your hunt, but if you do, send someone back and we'll come a'running!"

"Thanks Major, will do," answered Tate as he reined Shady away from the column and sat waiting for the wagons to catch up.

Sean greeted his pa with, "What was that all about?"

"Well, it seems the major had no idea just who he was sent out to protect! But once he found out about all these *influential* young men, he understood and gave me his card in case we need help."

"What good's a card gonna do if we get attacked by a bunch o' Sioux?" asked Sean, his remark eliciting laughter from Jacques and family.

"I dunno. Maybe we can wave it 'em and they'll tremble in fear at the thought of the boys in blue comin' to rescue us!" He laughed at the thought, as did the others that were within earshot.

THE WESTERN CLOUDS gathered like a chorus line to watch the horizon pull the sun toward its resting place. Long lances of pale gold and white shot heavenward and the brilliance outlined the dark clouds showing silver fringe. Tate watched the long column of blue point its way to the southwest for its return to the safety of the high walled fort. He had scouted the road ahead and found a wide grassy flat where the river turned back on itself and left its former course overgrown with deep grama. This would give the animals ample graze and he and Sean would have time to scout their next day's route before full dark.

. . .

T<small>ATE AND</small> S<small>EAN</small> were welcomed to the cookfire of the Bottineau family with Red Leaf directing them to be seated as she dipped their plates full of the hot stew. Fawn handed each a cup of coffee and seated herself next to Sean. The family had already had their fill, but they were pleased to have the company of Tate and son. Once Tate slowed his eating and reached for his coffee, Jacques asked, "You saw the sign of the herd, no?"

Tate nodded, swallowing the mouthful of java, and answered, "Yeah, but it looked to be at least a week old, don'tcha think?"

"*Oui, oui.* But it is the first sign of a large herd."

"Yup, an' I reckon they were headed north, up to the grasslands that are south of the Black Hills, at least that's according to Jim Baker. I ain't been around these parts too much, my home's quite a ways west o' here, in the Wind River Mountains. But, Jim did say up north o' here is where most o' them big herds like to summer. Seems there's a lot o' flatlands that are deep in buffalo grass, grama, an' the like. Prime doin's for buffler."

"*Mais Oui.* All this area is not too different from the plains of the northeast. More sage, and fewer trees, but still good country for the bison."

"When we scouted the trail ahead, the river cuts quite a canyon beyond here and we'll have to turn north anyway, so I figger we'll see 'bout that herd. It might just be the end of our trail an' these younkers can unlimber their rifles an' get a little experience with the woolies!"

Jacques grinned at his friend, chuckled a little and reached for a refill on his coffee. Tomorrow might be the beginning of an exciting experience, at least for the college boys.

CHAPTER TWENTY-THREE
LAKOTA

WITH AN EARLY START TATE HOPED TO MAKE IT OUT OF THE foothills and flat-tops. Baker told him about the Thunder Basin being a favorite grazing land for the big woolies, but he also said it was several days north of the Platte. Tate was counting on Baker's second choice when he said,

"There's another place I've seen 'em, bagged me some there too. If'n you head north from that wide flat by the Platte I tol' ya' 'bout, but keep the bigger hills off yore left shoulder and foller along the ridge some'r callin' the Haystacks. You'll come to a break that cuts back to the east and into the open. You might find 'em thar, but if'n not, keep to the north toward them Wildcat Hills an' you'll come to the headwaters of Muskrat Creek. That's a good place too." And if he was right, Tate knew they would have to make short work of getting ready. With time wasting, he wanted to make it to those flats before dark.

The route chosen held to the shoulder of the long sloping hillside well above the dry creek bottom. The greenery in the valley showed evidence of spring water, but not enough to give flow to a stream. As was common in the plains, the ravines and gullies had been carved by eons of summer storms that sent flash floods cascading through the hills to find the shortest and easiest escape from the torrents that chased the flows to lower lands. Their chosen route was through untraveled country. This was land known only to the natives and wildlife and had seldom, if ever, known the gaze of pioneers.

The buffalo grass and grama showed signs of grazing, but not recently. There was no churned earth to tell of the passing of buffalo herds, and the prickly pear and cholla were undisturbed. Juniper and piñon were scattered near the tops of the few hills and mesas, and the only wildlife the scouts kicked up were jackrabbits and coyotes. Sean shielded his eyes to watch a red-tailed hawk circling some prey below. When the bird tucked his wings to dive on its target, Sean reined up to watch. At the last instant, the bird started to spread its wings, then plucked his prey from the ground. Sean saw the squirming ball of fur and knew the hawk had taken a prairie dog. The fuzz-ball twisted and kicked, but the deep-sunk talons held firm and the hawk charted his course to the large stick nest in a cottonwood at the creek bottom. Sean cupped his hands to his mouth and mimicked the hawk with its extended whistling squeal. He was pleased to see the predator of the skies turn to look his direction, and Sean gigged Dusty forward to catch up to his pa.

"Talkin' to the birds again, eh?" asked his pa, chuckling at his grinning son.

"Sure Pa, ya never know when that'll come in handy." He had been practicing his mimicry since his childhood when he would walk around the clearing by their cabin listening to the birds of the woods and trying to make the same sounds. Sean had a sharp ear and could easily copy the calls of many animals with the only exception being the deep-throated growl of the grizzly.

As the valley narrowed, the trail dropped from the shoulder into the bottom to follow the dry creek bed. When a gap between the hills to the left showed another valley coming from the west, the trail was pushed away from the slope and into the deep sand. The first two wagons, smaller but both with a four-up hitch, gave the mules little concern as the wide wheels dug into the loose sand. When the trail rose to cross the long flat finger ridge, the mules clawed into the soil and pulled the wagons up the rise to top out on the flat. Both covered wagons made the crossing easily, but the freighters, though empty, were heavier and the wheels bore deeper. Bucky was standing in the extended box of the seat, cracking the whip over the heads of the mules. The whip sounded like a pistol shot each time the popper voiced its protest to the mules. With all four long-eared beasts leaning into their traces and digging deep, they struggled, lost their footing and gained it again, and the dried wood joints squeaked as the wagon box twisted to mount the side-sloping trial made by the others. Within moments, they topped out and pulled to the side to await the last wagon.

But the second freighter, though handled by an experienced teamster named Wilks, bogged down in the loosened sands. The wheels sunk over the rims, and the mules were digging deeper than their hocks. The whip cracked again and again, and the raspy voice of the teamster shouted commands and insults at the struggling dusty and sweating beasts. Lather was showing white under the harness, the mules had open mouths fighting the bits, water flowed from their eyes trying to wash the dust away, and finally the teamster gave in and sat back, letting the reins go slack on the backs of the mules.

Bucky hollered down to Wilks, "Rest 'em there! I'll hook mine up an we'll get'cha outta there!"

Wilks waved a tired hand, propped his foot on the edge of

the seat box and with elbow on knee, he heaved a heavy sigh and spoke softly to his mules. "Easy now boys, help'sa comin' and we'll get outta here right quick. Just stand easy, now." Two of the animals turned to see the driver, bending their necks almost completely around to see past the blinders, but their eyes told of their understanding, although they still nodded their heads as they protested the bits.

In a short while, Bucky was slowly backing his four-up hitch down the slope to join the teams below. He hooked the big doubletree to the long extended falling tongue, lined the team out and looked over his shoulder to Wilks, nodded, and both men cracked whips and hollered, "Hyahh, mules, pull!" All eight mules dug hooves into the loosened dirt, trace chains rattled, and teamsters kept shouting and snapping the whips, demanding more from the animals. The wheels began to move, and finally progress was made. Once moving, the wagon was hauled to the crest of the slope and halted.

From atop the slight rise, the narrowing of the valley's end could be seen, but the men chose to take an early nooning and the roustabouts gathered bits of sage, dead cottonwood that remained along the dry creek from wetter summers, and some old buffalo chips, to put together enough of a fire to put on some coffee. From far up the valley, the scouts, Tate, Sean, and Fawn, looked back from their promontory to see the wagons stopped, and decided to return.

"Pa, ya think them college boys'll be excited 'bout us findin' them buffalo?" asked Sean as the three mounted up to return. They had crested the rise at the north end of the Haystack buttes and glassed the wide plains beyond. There, no more than a mile or two, was a massive herd of buffalo lazily grazing on the flats. Sean was astounded at the numbers and as he gazed through the brass telescope, he let a low whistle escape, "Wow, Pa, there's gotta be thousands of 'em. I ain't never seen so many!"

"It's a good-sized herd alright. At least it'll be 'nuff to keep 'em busy for a while. Hopefully it won't take too long for 'em to get their fill of killin'," mused Tate, thinking of the task before them. He wanted the men to experience every gory detail of a big kill including the hard work of skinning and field-dressing the giants of the plains.

They had no sooner pointed their mounts back down the valley when a volley of gunfire racketed from below. Even from the distance they could see the puffs of smoke and the low-lying cloud of grey. At Tate's nod, the three dug heels to the ribs of their mounts and were off at a dead run, uncertain at what they would find, but without an obvious attack and no return fire, Tate was sure it hadn't come from Indians. As they rode up, the group of men, collegians and teamsters alike, were pointing to the high ridge and shouting, "Indians! Indians!" Tate looked near the big freighter and saw one of the slaves, the youngest named Timothy, lying near the front wheel with an arrow protruding from his neck. The man was obviously dead, but as Tate quickly searched the area, there were no other arrows or other sign of an attack.

He scowled at the big Teamster boss, Bucky, "How many?!"

"I didn't see nary a one! But that arrow came from up thataway!" he responded, pointing.

Jacques stepped to the side of Tate's horse looking up at his friend, "I was on the other side, I saw nothing but a puff of dust. I believe there was only one."

With a quick scan of the hill that Tate had scouted before, he turned to Sean, "Get 'em started to the end of the valley. If I'm not back by dusk, make camp at the end of the ridge, by the creek but on the other side."

"Sure, Pa."

Shady lunged forward, Lobo at his side, and within moments Tate had disappeared around the shoulder of the hill. He remembered this side valley having more juniper and piñon that would give him cover as he sought to come around the back side of the hill, and hopefully find the attackers. The hill stretched back to the west and Tate stayed on the downhill side of the willows and chokecherries that lined the bottom dry creek. Within a short distance, the ravine made an "s" bend to a saddle across the tail of the long hill. He reined up, surveying the open hillside for any movement. The red slashes on the south side showed remnants of long deteriorated mineral deposits, and the gradual slope to the valley floor was devoid of anything bigger than cholla.

With a simple hand signal Tate sent Lobo ahead, and he and Shady followed cautiously. As they neared the saddle crossing, Lobo trotted back to Tate, and quickly turned to lead him to the tracks of a fast-moving, unshod horse. He moved across the trail, scanning for more tracks, but there were none. Tate looked down at Lobo, now sitting on his haunches with his tongue lolling out and appearing to be smiling at his friend, and said, "Well, boy. Looks like there was only one. Shall we see if we can catch him?"

Lobo immediately took off on the trail and Tate had no excuse to not follow. He reached down and patted Shady on the neck, "Looks like we got it to do, boy. Let's go!"

The grulla took to the trail at a long-legged canter and Tate knew the horse could go like this for hours. But he had to be careful everytime they neared a crest or cluster of trees, anything that would provide the attacker cover to ambush Tate. For some distance, Tate saw the tracks showed the Indian was no longer fleeing at a run. *Could be his horse is gettin' tired, or he's lookin' for someplace to check his backtrail.*

At the crown of the next ridge, Tate approached the crest slowly. Stepped down from Shady and ground tied him, then hunkered down to reach the edge. He removed his hat and peered over to see juniper covered hillsides. Steep slopes dropped to a narrow valley below and more timber covered the opposite slope. Tate scampered back to his saddle bags for his scope and returned to the promontory. He chose a bit of a knob that was sheltered by a scraggly juniper and sat down to scope the opposite hill. It didn't take long to spot the lone Indian crouching behind a rocky talus ridge, obviously hoping to ambush his follower. With continued scanning, Tate planned his route to avoid any ambush and hopefully turn the tables on the attacker. Once decided, he scurried back to Shady, and with Lobo close at his side, they dropped off the hilltop on the north side to make their way across the valley just north of where the warrior was waiting.

"A HO!" shouted Tate as he stood above and behind the lone attacker. The Indian was startled and spun around bringing up his bow with nocked arrow.

"Don't!" shouted Tate, but the man let the arrow fly. Tate jumped to the side and dropped to his one knee, as the arrow whistled by, narrowly missing him. Tate had his rifle held on the man before he shot the arrow, but his sudden move prevented him from shooting, but Lobo would not be stayed. The big grey wolf sailed over a large boulder and struck the frightened Indian with all of his weight, taking the man to the ground. Lobo sunk his teeth into the man's shoulder strap next to his neck, and the man screamed.

"Lobo! Off! Off!" shouted Tate as he neared the pair. His rifle held at his hip, pointed at the downed man, "Here, Lobo, sit!" The wolf had released his grip, but was still atop the prone figure as he turned to look back at Tate. At the second command, the wolf gave one look and growl at the bloodied attacker and spun around to come to the side of Tate.

Another couple of steps brought Tate closer to the man, who scooted back from him, fear-filled eyes glaring and his hand holding the wound.

"English?" asked Tate.

A glaring stare was all the man gave.

"I am Longbow. Known by the Arapaho, Crow, and others," stated Tate, using the tongue of the Arapaho. But there was no recognition from the man who tried to scoot farther back but was stopped by another boulder.

Tate resorted to sign language and asked what tribe the man was from. He answered, "Lakota!"

Tate motioned to himself, "I am Longbow." Then pointed to the attacker.

"Plan-doo-ta," answered the man, grimacing from pain in his shoulder.

Tate motioned Lobo to lay down, leaned his rifle near the wolf on a boulder, and started for the downed Lakota. He signed, "I will bandage your shoulder, then we will go."

SEAN WAS the first to see them coming. Dusk had faded and the long shadows of approaching darkness followed the two riders into the camp. The Indian had a patch of buckskin bandage on one shoulder, his hands were bound, and his feet tied together with the long rawhide tether stretching under the horse's belly. He glared at the others as they gathered around, asking questions. Tate briefly explained, "Caught up with him, and Lobo took a chunk. He's Lakota."

Jacques stepped forward, looking at the man and spoke to him, in the language of the Dakota, "I am Jacques, this man is Longbow, what is your name?"

"Plan-doo-ta, Red Otter, I am Ogalala under Red Cloud of the Lakota!" he declared defiantly.

"Wal, I'll leave him in your hands, Jacques. See if you can

find out why he attacked us all by himself and whatever else he might be up to." He looked around and asked Red Leaf, "You got somethin' cookin' in your pot yonder you could share with me and that young'un," motioning to his captive. "He looks to be 'bout the same age as Sean, so I can't figger what he was doin' out by himself. But, I reckon he's hungry and he might talk a little better on a full stomach."

Red Leaf nodded and motioned him and Jacques to bring the Lakota to their fire.

CHAPTER TWENTY-FOUR
BUFFALO

ONCE RED OTTER WAS FILLED, HE DID NOT HESITATE TO DO all he could to berate the white men and their incursion into the land of his fathers. Once he began, he stood and stomped around, even with his hands still tied, and swung his arms about as he scowled and stared at the gathered crowd of white men. It was all Jacques could do to keep up with the translation, so all could understand.

"When my people signed the white man's paper at Fort Laramie we were promised the land would be ours 'as long as the river flows and the eagle flies,' but still your people came. When our leaders offered horses for one cow that was taken, your soldiers attacked. When we defended our village, they came again and killed two hands times two hands of our women. Now they would enter the land we say is holy, the Paha Sapa, and your long-knives do not stop them. You," he nodded his head, "bring big wagons to take our buffalo, so our people will go hungry. So, we fight!"

"Why were you out here alone?" asked Tate.

"I look for horses."

"By yourself? Where is your village?"

"Horses for price of woman, must take them alone," answeredOtter, stoically.

Tate grinned, looked at the others, "That explains a lot, he's got his eyes on a woman and wants to pay her father the bride price," chuckling. "Why did you attack us?" he added.

"To see if you were afraid. If you were, I could easily take the horses that followed."

Tate looked at the gathered group of collegians that sat around the fire, listening and watching the first close-up Indian they had seen. He explained to them, "Ain't it amazin' what some men'll do for a woman? Aren't you glad you don't have to go steal some horses, take some scalps, and more, all for the love of a woman?"

The men grinned and nodded their heads, but Patrick chimed in, "After what I've seen with some women and what some fellas do, there's not much difference, except for the scalping, of course!"

THERE WAS LITTLE LEFT to be said by the Lakota and he was bound to the front wheel of a freighter, but was given a blanket. The others turned in except for Jacques family and Tate that sat by the fire, discussing the plans for the coming days.

"How long you think we have before they send someone looking for him?" asked Tate.

"He told me this was his third day away, but his people know his quest, so, I do not think we can know how long they will wait. I think maybe three to five days, maybe more."

"Like I told you before, I want these young men to get involved in everything there is to know about takin' a buffalo. From shootin' to skinnin' to guttin' and smokin' the meat and tannin' the hides. And all that's gonna take time, time that I'm not sure we have if the Sioux come down on us. These boys need to know what the 'savages' as they're prone to call 'em, have to do to live out here. If they can understand what the natives do and how they have to live, maybe they'll use some of their influence for good."

"I would like to see that as well, my friend, but I don't think it will happen," answered Jacques, shaking his head. "*Non*, I do not. These young men have been *choyé,* uh, how you say, pampered all their lives, and even if they do learn about the buffalo, I think when they go back to the city, they will forget the people of the plains."

"I'm afraid you're right, Jacques. But the only reason I took this job was in hopes that maybe some of 'em would understand that what the politicians preach is a long way from the truth of things."

"*Oui,* you are right my friend, but . . . " and he left the thought hanging in the smoke of the cookfire.

THE FIRST HINT of light showed as a thin strip at the eastern horizon when Tate began stationing the grumbling would-be hunters for their first buffalo shoot. Tate and Sean had scouted the area well and knew exactly where the men needed to be to get more than one shot at a buffalo. Although the scattered herd stretched as far east and north as they could see, Tate knew that if they were spooked enough to stampede, it might take several days to catch up and finish the hunt. There would be six shooters, not counting Jacques, Tate, and Sean. Tate was counting on Jacques and his women to direct the skinning and dressing of the animals that would mostly be done by the teamsters and roustabouts, with a little help from the Yale boys. And now he and Sean were stationing the shooters as they previously planned.

Straight west of their camp was a cluster of bald hills that offered little graze, while a dry wash cut across the flat in that direction. North of the wash, dusty green marked the wide flat that was the chosen graze for the herd and farther north stretched the flats. Tate believed that by putting the shooters in the wash, they would have good cover and if the buffalo spooked, they would continue north in the flats. Sean took Clifton Burge with his Sharps, Louis Reale who was armed with his Dreyse Needle rifle, and Robert Wooster, who was more interested in writing about the hunt than shooting but carried a .54 caliber Hawken. They rode into the slow rising sun and had their faces painted with the bright colors of red and orange as the sun made its first peek over the flat horizon. Sean stationed the men at about twenty-yard intervals, with Burge anchoring the end of the line. He explained, as did Tate, that he would be near in the event that anyone needed any help, then ground tied his appy in the deep draw and climbed to the edge to watch the buffalo.

Tate had Patrick Hutton anchor the near end of the line and placed Justis and Smits toward the center. He had instructed each man about taking only cows without calves and or young bulls. "Them big'uns ain't good eatin' and they're almighty big to get the skin off."

The signal for the first shot would come from Tate's pistol and the shooters were told if they take more than two buffalo each, they would have to single-handedly skin and gut every other animal downed. But he also knew they had no idea what kind of work that would mean, so he thought some of them would not let up on their shooting until they were out of ammunition.

When the long rays of the rising sun bent their way across the flats, the sight of thousands of buffalo was mesmerizing to the newcomers from the east. Many were laying down with their legs folded before them, chewing their cud and lifting their heads slightly to the rising sun. Others were staggering to their feet, starting an early search for their daily graze. Most were standing, heads bowed, still in their drowse.

The single shot from Tate's Dragoon exploded, bouncing back from the hills behind them, startling the shooters more than the buffalo. But the men did not hesitate long, as the big rifles sounded again and again. Tate watched as some of the animals dropped as if their legs had been jerked from under them, and others stepped off, staggered, and fell. At the first loud report from a Sharps, every animal on the south side of the herd jerked slightly at the shocking sound, and the animals moved as one, starting at a trot into the sun, following the lead bull. But Sean fired the Spencer into the dirt just in front of it, turning him back on the others. The tide turned, and the brown wave swung back toward the west, and Tate gave them a short lead before firing in front of the lead cow, who also swung to the side, turning the herd back on itself once again. Once more, Sean fired the big Spencer, kicking dirt just in front of the bull, who turned back again. However, this time, the confused animals that were seldom frightened by anything, began milling to a stand. Several started trotting away, but did not go far as they sought the shelter of the herd. Cows with calves started bellowing for the copper colored offspring that came running, probably thinking they were getting their morning's rations.

The shooting grew more sporadic as the cloud of smoke hung heavy before the shooters. Most had heeded the orders about taking no more than two, but Tate heard the distant report of the Sharps of Clifton Burge. It was not surprising to Tate that he was the one that thought it alright to shoot as many as he could. A man that bragged about his relation to the Vice-President also thought himself immune from discipline or any correction. But with no one else shooting even his Sharps fell silent.

Tate mounted Shady and with a wave to Sean, both men started for the herd. They had explained the necessity of making sure the animals were dead before approaching them on foot and now the two were moving among the carcasses to dispatch the wounded. Both men carried their Spencers and Sean was the first to shoot a wounded bull. Tate had to do-in two wounded cows, but he was satisfied he did not see any orphaned calves. Tate took one last look and stood in his stirrups to wave the waiting freighters forward.

After nervously milling around for a good while, the rest of the herd had moved off a couple hundred yards, but several of the old bulls had positioned themselves on the south edge of the herd and were watching the men while guarding the rest of the herd. Tate stood in his stirrups to wave the shooters out of the wash to help the skinners and others. At the signal, Jacques and the women also started toward the flats. While the others mounted up, Patrick and Justis climbed from the wash and started on foot toward the closest kills near the draw. Both men were reloading as they walked. With the Merrill Carbine of Justis actually an early version manufactured by Remington, it was not a common weapon although a single-shot breech-loader using similar paper cartridges to the Sharps. But Justis was fumbling with the breech on the unfamiliar weapon and stopped to fix the problem. Patrick finished loading his Sharps, but was distracted by his friend as he fussed with his rifle. As Patrick turned to go back to help his friend, he heard the thunder of approaching hooves and looked up to see a big bull, head swinging and slobber flying, come charging directly at them from a cloud of dust.

Patrick hollered, "Look out! Look out!" frantically pointing at the charging bull that was lumbering more toward Justis. Patrick lifted his Sharps and drew a quick bead on the thundering monster, pulled the trigger, and the rifle bellowed its bark. But the bull did not slow nor stumble, and Justis turned to run, dropping his rifle as he started back towards the wash.

The shouting and the blast of the Sharps caught Sean's attention and he instantly whirled the appy around to give chase to the bull. Coming at an angle toward the bull, the long-legged Appaloosa stretched out with Sean leaning low on his neck. With the Spenser resting across the pommel, Sean and Dusty gained on the bull but the beast was too near the man. The bull bellowed, lowered his massive head and caught Justis between his horns and tossed the man like a limp doll over his head to land in a heap behind him. The buffalo started to make a wide swing to return to his target, but Sean was too close, and the sudden blast of the Spencer took the bull just behind the front leg and the massive woolie's head dropped between his legs and the one-ton monster flipped over on his back, rolled to his side and lay still.

Sean jacked the lever to reload the big rifle as he reined Dustyto a slow stop. He looked back to see the bull on its side, dust rising from the ruckus. Sean breathed deep, dropped his shoulders and felt his hand tremble. He looked to see if anyone saw and grabbed at the reins and held to the saddle horn to steady himself. He heard the rumble of hooves and looked to see his pa canter near, rein to a stop, and look at his son.

Tate grinned ear to ear, "That was sumpin'," he drawled in a typical Tate understatement. He nodded his head and said, "Let's go see to that fella that got hit, what say?"

"Sounds reasonable," said Sean, hoping his voice wouldn't crack with the shakes he was feeling.

CHAPTER TWENTY-FIVE
WAR PARTY

SPOTTED TAIL WAS SEATED ACROSS THE FIRE FROM TWO OF THE prominent chiefs of the Lakota, Little Thunder and Iron Shell. Beside them sat the sub-chief, Crow Dog and seated nearby were elders, the village medicine man, and several other warriors. It was the council of the Sičháŋǧu Oyáte, or Brulé band of the Sioux. It was a somber gathering as the village mourned the loss of the warriors of Spotted Tail's band, but the leader had to give an accounting before the chiefs and elders.

A thin spiral of smoke sought exit from the smoke flaps at the top of the hide lodge and the wailings of the mothers and women of the warriors had carried on for several days, continuing throughout the night and the morning. Little Thunder sat cross-legged and stared sternly at the man before him. Spotted Tail had become a respected warrior and war leader of the people and had never failed before. Many had thought he would rise to be one of their great chiefs, but now even his position as a sub-chief was questioned. Spotted Tail had finished his account of the fight with the whites of the wagons and now sat silent, waiting for the decision of the council. Although they had talked for some time before re-admitting Spotted Tail to the lodge, there were questions remaining.

"Did you see these rifles that shoot many times?" asked Little Thunder.

"What I heard was many shots from the same place. What I saw did not look different than other rifles."

"How many had these rifles?" queried Iron Shell.

"Four men came from cover, all with rifles," he dropped his head, "I believe there were others that did not show themselves."

"Our friend, Kicking Bear, of the Ogalala, knows of these wagons. Even now they come into our lands to hunt buffalo. It is the decision of this council that you will go with Crow Dog and with three hands of warriors, you will take these wagons and return with the rifles that shoot many times. When you do this, you will be restored to your position as a sub-chief among the people," declared Little Thunder. It was left unsaid, but understood, what the consequences would be if the mission failed.

WHITE HAWK, the woman of Spotted Tail's lodge, stood beside his horse holding her man's hand and looking up at the father of her two children. "Do not fail, my husband, your children and I will be waiting. If you must bring something, bring meat for our lodge, I do not need any help." It was her subtle way of saying there was no place for another woman in her lodge, for she knew that was what had caused him to suffer the defeat at the hands of the whites.

He had tried to tell her the captive was to be her helper, to save her from such hard work, but she knew the captive was for him. She had seen other warriors bring a second or third wife to the lodge because they believed it strengthened their stand and respect among other warriors, but White Hawk knew the first wives always resented having to share their lodge with younger women. Even captive women that had no rights and were treated as slaves still caused problems with a man and his woman. She fingered the knife at her belt, withdrew it slightly from the scabbard, making sure that Spotted Tail saw the movement, and smiled at her man. The subtle threat was obvious to him and he knew she was capable of anything that would suit her purpose.

"I will have no time for captives. We only seek to take the rifles of the white man," he explained, eyeing her hand on the knife. White Hawk had proven herself a capable warrior and could have followed the warrior path, but chose to be with Spotted Tail. If he saw her as a warrior, he knew she could as easily raise his scalp as that of a captive.

"That is good," answered White Hawk, a grin tugging at one corner of her mouth as she looked sidelong at Spotted Tail. She released his hand and stepped back as he reined around to join the others led by Crow Dog.

THE CAMP of the Brulé was well south of the Niobrara River and up against the north end of the Wildcat Hills. Where their Ogalala friend, Kicking Bear, had reported the white buffalo hunters were camped was in the lower end of the flats. It would take more than a day of travel for the war party to reach the white man's camp and to prepare for their attack. Kicking Bear would not be with them on the hunt, choosing instead to court a prospective bride he had met at the summer gathering of the people for the sun dance.

With two advance scouts before them, Spotted Tail and

Crow Dog rode together at the head of the war party. Crow Dog looked at the man he had respected for so long and asked, "Why did the white man let you go?"

"He said the captive was his son and he had him back, so he saw no need for more killing."

"You said there were two captives?"

"Yes, a young man and woman. They were together when we took them."

"But the woman was not his?" asked Crow Dog, trying to understand this white man they would go against.

"No, she was Dakota. Her people were to the far north and east, but her father was a Métis, and he was with the others."

They rode in silence for a good distance before Spotted Tail spoke again, "The white man, he is called Longbow."

Crow Dog reined his horse to a stop, looked over at Spotted Tail, "Longbow? I have heard of a man with the Arapaho called Longbow! They say he is a great warrior with the bow. Is this the one?"

Spotted Tail slowly nodded, "He shot several arrows from a distance," and he looked around at the nearby hills, "as far as that tree on the ridge." The tree he pointed at was over two hundred yards away and Crow Dog stared at the tree and back at Spotted Tail.

"No man can shoot an arrow that far!" declared Crow Dog, motioning to the distant point.

"He did, several times. I did not believe until his son placed a blanket on a bush and he shot it."

With a doubting look to Spotted Tail, the man shook his head and started again on the dim trail across the flat-topped butte. As they neared the edge of the butte, their scouts rode up from the bottom through a narrow draw and topped out just before the group. Crow Dog conversed with the scouts as the others drew near, then he announced they would drop off the butte to the valley below and make camp. "We will reach the camp of the whites before midday. We will catch them at their meal and it will be easy to take them while they eat."

CHAPTER TWENTY-SIX
AFTERMATH

THE FINAL TALLY OF THE INITIAL HUNT WAS TWELVE ANIMALS down. Bucky and the roustabouts set to work immediately on the dressing out of the carcasses with Jacques and Red Leaf giving instructions to the six collegians. Tate was surprised and pleased to see every one of the young men, even the bruised and very sore Justis, as well as the three slaves, responding and doing their share and more of the work. Even Sean and Fawn, with the supervision of both Lobo and Indy, were busy deboning the large hind quarters and stacking the meat on the laid-out hides. It was a busy crowd and Tate separated himself to a promontory on the shoulder of the hill above their camp, to watch for anyone and anything that might pose a threat to the workers and the bounty.

And there were other volunteers, uninvited though they were, that were assisting in the clean-up. Gut piles had attracted coyotes, foxes, badgers, ravens, magpies, whiskey jacks, and turkey buzzards. There were a few hawks and eagles on a couple of the fresher piles, but when the crowds of carrion eaters moved in, the more noble of the birds would take their morsels and return to their perches or nests, as there was more than enough for everyone and it served no purpose to fight over the scraps. When three lean wolves trotted to the crowd at the farthest pile, the lesser foragers scattered and surrendered their feast to the larger beasts.

It was late afternoon when the two freighters rolled back into camp. Red Leaf and Fawn had already crafted several meat racks from the willows by the narrow stream that cut their camp. Sean and Jason Biddle had been given the task of gathering the dried cottonwood and any other well dried wood, except for pine, for firewood for the smoke racks. Red Leaf had all the young hunters busy at the lowered tailgates of the freighters, cutting the meat into long thin strips for the drying and smoking. The cutters kept the women busy stringing the strips on the drying racks and Jacques had recruited two of the young hunters to assist him. He had been tasked with hanging several hind quarters high in the nearby aspens, well out of reach of the bigger predators and within the quaking leaves to discourage the feathered foragers.By sacking and hanging the meat, the cool breezes of the valley would start the curing.

As they started the smoke fires, the stripped leg bones were stacked around the edge \to roast the bones and marrow for use in pemmican. The teamsters and roustabouts had been given charge of the hides, with the exception of those used to keep the meat off the ground, and were scraping the remaining flesh before hanging the cleaned hides on the sides of the freighters to dry.

From Tate's promontory outlook, he could see the length of the valley back the way they came as well as the more narrow and thicker timbered upper reaches. Across the valley were the sparsely timbered hillsides that rose to the long flat mesa and other buttes that stretched out to the north. He was ready to return to camp and enjoy some fresh buffalo tongue and loin that he smelled cooking, but chose to take one last long look around, using his scope before the fading light of dusk shrouded the flatlands. He scanned the flats and the still milling herd, then turned his attention to the long line of hills that pointed north to the bald slopes beyond. As he turned to the upper end of the valley, movement caught his attention. He lowered the scope, and slowly watched the scattered juniper and piñon. His father taught him, "If you wanna see somethin', don't look directly at it. You'll see motion before anything, and then whatever is different will stand out, but only to your peripheral vision."

There! Movement among the trees at the edge of the long flat-top mesa across the valley. Once he located the spot, he lifted his scope and searched. Two Indians, probably Sioux, were mounting to leave. Tate knew immediately they were scouts, probably for a much larger band, maybe a hunting or even a war party. As the two horsemen disappeared behind the thicker timber, he thought. *They could be searching for our captive friend, or they could be with the one, Spotted Tail, that I let go after we got Sean and Fawn back. Either way, it's trouble.*

He walked off the sloping shoulder back to the camp. With darkness settling in, the women were busy at the cookfire. Red Leaf had boiled a tongue, taken it from the pot and sliced it, and now the pieces were frying in fresh fat grease. Slices of steak hung over the flames, skewered on long willow withes. Tate's stomach grumbled its impatience and Jacques extended a cup of coffee to his friend.

"You look troubled, my friend, what is it?" asked Jacques.

"Spotted a couple Sioux scouts, across the valley yonder. I'm purty sure they were scoutin' our camp."

Jacques lifted his head slightly as he considered, "Friends of the boy, Red Otter?"

"Or maybe Spotted Tail returning for his revenge," surmised Tate.

"When?"

"I'm thinkin' some time tomorrow. The scouts have to return to the party, then they have to come up and . . . well, maybe check things out themselves, figger when to hit us that'll be most effective, you know. . ."

"What are you thinking, I mean, about what we should do?" queried the Métis.

They were interrupted by Red Leaf, "Food is ready." She was busy at the fire, retrieving the steaks and setting the frying pan on the nearby rocks. Tate, Jacques, and Sean accepted plates from Fawn and started stacking the fare. Everyone savored the fresh buffalo, especially the tender and tasty fried tongue.

As they sat back to enjoy their coffee, Jacques looked at the thoughtful Tate and waited his plan.

"Well, the way I see it, I don't think they'll hit us first thing in the mornin', and if not, we'll have time to set up some defenses. We might oughta let everyone know of the possibility, but as far as keepin' watch, I don't think I'd really wanna trust anybody but us three," he pointed to Sean, Jacques, and himself.

"*Oui*, I agree. But with these hills behind us, it would be easy to bring a surprise attack and we would have a hard time defending."

"You're right about that, Jacques, but I don't want us too far out in the open. I prefer to have some control or advantage."

"Pa, why don't we just move the wagons out a little way, circle 'em up, but, make it look like we ain't expectin' nothin', you know, be busy an' such," suggested Sean.

"*Oui*, and maybe we could surprise them!" added Jacques.

"That's a start, anyway. An' if they don't come early, we'll have time to take some cover back on these finger ridges and such, but that'll have to wait till mornin'." He chuckled a little,

"An' these college boys ain't gonna like doin' more work. I'm thinkin' most of 'em did more today than at any other time in their lives."

Jacques grinned at the comment and added, "*Mais Oui,* and even with the stink of buffalo on 'em, they were too tired to clean up. They just rolled up in their blankets and started snoring."

"Well, maybe we and the teamsters can get the wagons moved and let them fellas wake up and see the wagons gone an' see what they do!"

CHAPTER TWENTY-SEVEN
SIOUX

THE STARS WERE SNUFFING THEIR LANTERNS AND THE CLOAK of darkness was retreating toward the western mountains as Tate sat beside a scrub piñon, cracking the handful of nuts gathered from the cones on its branches. The thin shelled delicacy that was only offered every five or six years, was a tasty tidbit he often enjoyed in his private moments with his God. He was near the crest of the highest hill in this range, with the long line of round-tops stretching to the north a little more than three miles. At the left edge was a long formation that could only be described as a double valley. Tate thought it looked as if the Creator formed two equal rows in His garden between the parallel lines of hilltops and flat-topped buttes. Beyond these formations, the hills jogged to the west and the valley opened to wide grasslands.

He had mounted this same hill a few hours after dark to search for any pinpoints of light that would tell of a camp, and he was disappointed although not surprised. It would have been uncharacteristically careless of the war party to have a fire that would give away their location, but he thought maybe their overconfidence in their strength would make them a little less wary. When it was time for Jacques to relieve Sean at his guard, Tate descended the hilltop to catch a little sleep before he was awakened to stand his turn. Now, once again atop the hill, he communed with his God as he watched for signs of the Sioux.

With a minimum of movement, and even that masked by the nearness of the piñon, he repeatedly searched the distance for any movement. As he looked to the camp below, he also tried to put himself in the mind of the leader of the attackers and thought of what he would do to attack the group below. The possible approaches would be from the flats where the herd still grazed, down the valley between the ridges, between the hills where the wagons came from the south, or over the tops and finger ridges. The type of cover usually preferred by the Indian if attacking on foot would be where the juniper and piñon sporadically covered the hill-sides. But if coming on horseback in an all-out charge, it would probably come from the cut in the hills that held the road used by the wagons, or perhaps from the flats to try to drive them back into the valley into a waiting ambush. He grinned as he thought of the last, knowing it was a favorite attack of the plains Indians.

With another search of the upper valley and the flat-tops across the way, he looked back at the terrain below, calculating where to place shooters. The camp was in a natural basin with the hill at their back, but that made it susceptible to attackers coming over the finger ridge behind them. He searched for natural cover, good shooting positions, and alternate places. As his plan began to form, he scratched it in the dirt at his feet, reviewing all the possibilities as he adjusted.

A deep growl from the grey wolf at his side, turned Tate around to see what had alarmed Lobo. It was a moment before he saw them. But when he saw the Sioux at the head of the double bottomed valley, they were lined out single file, moving among the trees in the closer of the two draws. He watched with his scope, trying to count but the dim light hindered. He dropped the scope, looking around for any other movement and caught a glimmer of motion at the edge of the flat-top mesa, right near the tree line. More Sioux, but a smaller group. The band of grey light of early morning did little to help Tate to make out those in the bottom of the valley, but those atop the mesa were easily seen as the rising sun struggled to climb above the flat-lined horizon in the east. They were still about three or four miles away, and he had to get his shooters readied. Another scan with the scope at the bigger group and he guessed their number to be at least ten with the other about six or seven.

Tate slid back away from the crest, turned and trotted down the hillside, being careful to watch his steps, not wanting to slide in the gravel and kick up a dust cloud that would warn the Sioux. Sean saw his dad coming, spoke to Jacques, Bucky, and Patrick and the four stepped forward to hear his warning. Within moments, he outlined what he believed would be the plan of attack, "Jacques, I want you and one shooter, you choose, on that finger ridge yonder. You'll see the larger group coming and you can signal the others. Don't shoot until they start their attack. Patrick, you need to place your shooters among the wagons, making sure they have good line of sight and cover, and if you have any extra rifles, arm the slaves as well.

"Bucky, you split your roustabouts with you and Wilks, half on this side on the face of this hill and likewise over yonder. Make sure they have good cover. From up there, you'll have the attackers in a cross fire with the shooters in the wagons so make sure you don't kill any o' them college boys! Alright now, everybody git! Them Sioux will be here pretty quick now!"

"Jacques!" Tate hollered to get the Métis attention, and motioned him back. As he drew close, "Make sure your women are well armed. But, I want them visible at the tailgates of the wagons, lookin' busy and not paying attention. I want the Sioux to think they've surprised us, but make sure they are in a good covered spot when the shooting starts."

He grinned, "It is clear your woman is not here, for you would know to tell a woman what to do at a time like this is useless! They will do right, you'll see!"

Tate turned to Sean and pointed out the location he was to take higher up the hill on the south side of the cut where the second wave of attackers would be expected to come. "I'll be over there," he pointed across the way on the opposite hillside. "After the first attack comes, they'll expect the group to fall back into this notch where the horses are," he pointed to the cutback that held the horses behind a brush barrier. "But when they don't, then the others will come through here to attack from the rear. Don't start shooting until they are all in the bottom here, or better yet, wait till I shoot. You probably won't need them, but make sure you have a couple tubes of cartridges close by. Also, there's a place up there where you can keep your appy tethered and out of the way, just in case you need him. I'll have Shady with me also. Alright?"

"Sure Pa, I understand. But, do you think the women will be alright?"

Tate couldn't keep from letting a grin start at one corner of his mouth, but dropped his head and put his hand on his son's shoulder, "Son, we'll just have to trust that she'll be fine."

TATE WAS in position high on the hill and watching as a single scout from each group separated from the others and kept to as much cover as possible, scouting the wagons. Tate had signaled his men to stay under cover and watched as the scouts returned to their respective groups to report.

The four wagons formed a diamond with the two freighters in a point toward the plains and the two smaller wagons toward the cut between the hills. In the center was a central cookfire, tended by the slaves, with big pots hanging over the coals and men sitting nearby. Patrick stood at the end of the freighters, watching the flats and keeping a close watch on Jacques, waiting for his signal the attack was coming.

————

SPOTTED TAIL WAS GIVEN the lead of the larger group and with the expected report, he did not hesitate as he signaled his warriors. They started at a trot toward the end of the finger ridge that obscured the wagons from view, but as they neared the end, Spotted Tail raised his rifle over his head and signaled as he slapped his legs to his mount and the charge began.

WHEN JACQUES WAVED TO PATRICK, he hollered to the men, "Now!" and every man instantly jumped to his feet and ran to his designated spot where his rifle waited. Although all the weapons of the men were effective long-range rifles, they were told to hold their fire until the attackers were near and to wait for Patrick's signal to begin firing. Red Leaf and Fawn had both jumped into the same freighter and were crouching below the sides, each with her Hawken at the ready. Within seconds, the screaming Sioux were charging in a wide spread line and an overanxious Patrick fired the first shot and a horse fell forward, throwing its rider over his head. At Patrick's shot, the others opened up, and the volley surprised the attackers as the roar of eight rifles thundered and spat their smoke and fire. Other horses were hit, stumbled and lost their riders, at least two attackers were struck and fell from their mounts.

The warriors answered with their own rifles and the racketing of the shots intermixed with the shouted war cries and screams caused a melee of confusion among the frightened collegians. Each man struggled to reload, and hurriedly took aim for another shot. Blood blossomed on the chest of a warrior just before Patrick as he tumbled over the rump of his charging horse. Louis Reale shouted when he hit a warrior that had staggered to his feet after his mount was shot from under him. Reale quickly inserted another paper cartridge in his Needle Gun and searched for another target. He knew he wasn't very good at hitting a moving target, but he waited and watched, until one warrior spun his horse around to start another charge and Reale took quick aim and fired. The warrior bent backwards, but wasn't unseated and sat up to scream at the wagons and charge again. Reale froze at the sight and heard a Hawken explode almost in his ear and he saw the warrior fall. Louis turned to the side and saw a smiling Fawn lowering her Hawken to reload.

One man, Robert Wooster, dropped his weapon and backpedaled towards the center of the circle, eyes wide and hands flailing as he sought cover and or escape, but there was none. The movement behind him caused Horatio, the older slave to spin around and see the younger man in a panic and trying to scream out his fear. Horatio trotted over to him, tried to calm him and finally had to slap the man back to reality. Wooster stared incensed at the black man and said, "How dare you!"

"Massa, you gots to get yo' gun and shoot the Indians!" shouted Horatio, pointing to the attackers. Everywhere he looked, men were firing at the mounted attackers that had split and were now on all sides of the wagons, running their mounts around the wagons as they sought to kill the hated white men.

Suddenly the teamsters opened fire from the hillsides and the Indians were startled when they realized they were in a crossfire. Bucky grinned as he struggled to reload, knowing his first shot had scored a hit and dropped an attacker on his belly. He had instructed the others to stagger their shots, and as soon as he was reloaded, he timed his to again score a hit, but this time a horse staggered and fell, and the rider tumbled against another downed warrior.

Spotted Tail saw the toll the rifles of the white men were taking on his men and he shouted to the warriors to follow as he led them away toward the flat. They left behind half of their number and as they reined up and swung around to look back at the wagons, Tail looked at his men, all with hangdog, even angry, expressions, and back at the wagons. Two horses of his men were trailing their reins as they stumbled away from the melee. A cloud of thin smoke hung just at wagon top, and was slowly dissipating. Suddenly, a barrage of rifle fire came from beyond the wagons and Spotted Tail grinned, "Crow Dog is attacking! We must go again!" he shouted as he taunted his men with his upraised rifle and slapped his legs to his horse to start his charge. The others screamed their war cries and followed their leader.

THE VOLLEY HEARD by Spotted Tail was indeed the attack by Crow Dog, but not with the effect they planned. The bend in the cut between the hills gave the Sioux chief the cover he wanted, but only from those in the wagons. As soon as they reached the point near the bend, Tate fired and the last man in the group was shot from his horse. Sean's rifle answered and also scored a hit. The others looked frantically, trying to find the shooters and as their horses sidestepped and nervously fought the bits, another warrior was blasted from his horse. Crow Dog shouted to the remaining two and they put their horses in a run toward the wagons, trying to escape the deadly fusillade from the hillsides. But before they made it to the wagons, another one fell to the fire from the Spencer in the hand of Sean.

The firing from the hillsides behind them had also diverted the attention of those by the wagons, and Louis Reale stood on the hub of the wheel of the freighter to look back. As his foot slipped, he grabbed at the side of wagon, looking around just in time to see the muzzle blast from the rifle in the hands of Spotted Tail. Reale fell back, his face blackened by the blast. Fawn looked to see the man when suddenly, an arm wrapped around her neck and jerked her over the side of the wagon, throwing her across the withers of a horse in front of the rider. Spotted Tail screamed his war cry, and spun his horse to return to the flats away from the wagons.

Red Leaf scrambled to the seat of the freighter, took aim at the fleeing man that had grabbed her daughter and started to shoot, but stopped herself as she saw her daughter's hair by the man's leg. Fearful of hitting Fawn, she lifted her eyes to the finger ridge where Jacques was and tried to signal, but he did not see the waving rifle. Leaf looked around for other attackers, seeing none near, she took aim at the rockpile where her man was firing and fired her rifle. The splat of the bullet on the rock behind him caught Jacques' attention and he looked for the shooter. Then he saw his woman, waving her arms frantically and pointing to the fleeing warrior. Jacques looked and saw the man with his captive laying across the withers of his horse, recognizing the long hair of his daughter.

Crow Dog and his one remaining warrior ran the

gauntlet of deadly fire from the teamsters on the hillside and the shooters behind the wagons, the warrior jerked with the strike of a bullet, but held to his mount. When Dog caught up with Spotted Tail, he saw the grinning man with his captive, still belly down across the withers of his horse. Only two warriors and two additional riderless horses were with Spotted Tail, the others having fallen to the withering fire of the men of the wagons.

"You were to get the rifles that fire many times, not a woman!" shouted Crow Dog.

"Who wants a rifle when you can have a woman such as this!" he declared as he put his hand at the small of Fawn's back.

"You are a coward! You could not fight. Your men are dead, and you think you have done something! You are nothing!" screamed Fawn, slapping at the man's leg.

TATE AND SEAN quickly mounted and rode to the wagons, where Red Leaf ran up to them, "They have taken Fawn!" she pointed to the Sioux sitting their horses at a distance.

Tate looked, reached into his saddle bags for his scope, motioned for Sean to take a seat atop the freighter. Sean quickly grabbed his Spencer, hopped onto the wagon seat and looked back at his pa.

"Take the one on the far right. The spotted horse in the middle has Fawn, but you can take the one on the right easy."

Sean propped his foot on the wagon box, dropped his elbow to his knee and took a careful aim with the big Spencer. He drew in a breath, held the sight on the top edge of the warrior's shoulder, let out a bit of breath and slowly squeezed the trigger. The big .56-56 Spencer bucked and belched as it roared. Smoke chased the bullet on its way and it found its mark, knocking the warrior from his horse, spooking the animal and startling the warriors, who turned and stared at the wagons, wide-eyed that they could shoot that far. They had purposely positioned themselves far beyond what they believed any rifle could shoot effectively and now they saw this man shot down.

"Aiieee," shouted Crow Dog and slapped his legs to his horse's ribs and started for the hills to the north at a run. He was followed by the others, including Spotted Tail and his captive.

"Pa! They're running! We've gotta get her back!" Sean jumped astride his appy, and dug his heels into the long-legged stallion's ribs. The spotted horse humped his back and lunged forward and within no more than two lengths was at a full run. Tate hollered to Jacques as he was running toward the wagons, "They've got Fawn, come on!"

It took a few moments for Jacques to get his mount saddled, and Leaf had grabbed a bag of pemmican, handing it to him as he swung aboard. She shouted, "Bring her back," as she watched her man give chase to the others.

CHAPTER TWENTY-EIGHT
CHASE

SEAN LEANED LOW ALONG DUSTY'S NECK, THE DARK MANE whipping at his face as he reached down to pat him on the neck, speaking encouraging words, as he slapped his legs against the stallion's ribs, demanding more. The long-legged Appaloosa stretched his head out, his mouth shut as tight as possible on the bit, tail flying in the wind, running like he loved it with his hooves pounding a staccato on the disappearing ground beneath. Water filled Sean's eyes and he wiped his face with his buckskin sleeve, struggling through squinted eyes to see the fleeing Sioux.

He knew Dusty wanted to run and Sean gave him his head. The big appy was fresh, hadn't stretched his legs in a few days, and he sensed the horses ahead of them must be caught. Sean knew the mounts of the raiders had to be tired and one carried double. He remembered his pa said one of the other warriors was wounded, and they were in pursuit of four desperate men. The appy had his stride and Sean knew they were gaining, with every stretch of those long legs his pride in his horse grew. "That's it boy, keep it up, we're gainin' on 'em!"

Sean twisted around to see behind him, and the dusty image of his pa reassured him. He had heard his pa call out to Jacques and knew the Métis would not be far behind. He thought of Fawn, feeling her fear and anger, knowing she would be doing everything possible to get free,but he also knew there was little the woman could do, carried as she was over the withers of the warrior's horse. As he thought of her, the drumming hoofbeats faded and he remembered when they were taken before, the look on the chief's face when he stared at Fawn. Then he realized, this was the same man! Sean remembered the glare when the warrior taunted him before, the same stare that showed when he turned back at the shot that dropped the man at his side! Spotted Tail! Sean ground his teeth at the thought that this man once again had Fawn, the muscles in his cheeks so tight he had to shout to release them, "Go boy! Go!" It was as if the big stallion found new strength, his front legs seemed to reach farther, his pace quickened, as Sean felt the saddle horn in his gut as he lay along the appy's neck.

Abruptly the Sioux took to a trail that mounted the slope of the hill, a trail that twisted through the juniper and pointed to the saddle between the knobs. Their horses were digging deep as they fought their way up the rocky trail. The raiders were about half way up the hillside when Sean and Dusty split the junipers, and the mountain horse took the trail in long humping leaps. As Sean looked at the deep dug-out tracks before him, he felt a sudden blow to his side, like he had been hit with a hot poker as he grabbed at the saddle horn and put his hand to his side. He looked at his hand, red with blood, and he realized for the first time in his life he had been shot! But Dusty didn't slow and Sean breathed deep, thinking only of Fawn. He knew he had to hang on; her life depended on him staying after the captors.

He broke through the timber as he crested the saddle

crossing, seeing the warrior frantically trying to reload his rifle. Without a thought, Sean pointed Dusty at the man on one knee and the big stallion trampled him under foot. He pushed his appy on without even looking back. He had felt the big horse stumble just a step as he knocked the man into the rocks, but Sean knew his pa would make certain that attacker would not fight again. Sean thought, *Now there's three!*

The trail ducked into the scraggly juniper and piñon, the short-needled branches slapping at Sean and Dusty, and the big horse jumping and dodging the rock-strewn path as they dropped from the top of the hills into the double valley below. At the valley bottom, Sean brought Dusty to a sliding stop when he saw the deep fresh tracks of the Sioux split with two horses going to each side of the low ridge in the middle of the valley floor. He jumped down to examine the tracks, first those on the near side, then running to the others he dropped to one knee to look closely at those. He stood, looking from one trail to the other, and heard the rattle of hooves on the trail behind him. "Pa! They split! Which one do we take?"

Tate dropped to the ground to examine the tracks, the quick look from the experienced tracker showed, "That one! Deeper tracks, he's carryin' double!"

Both men swung into their saddles as the horses started the pursuit. Sean was in the lead with the big stallion's longer strides. Tate breathed deep, watching his son holding tight to the saddle horn. He had seen the blood on Sean's shirt and knew he had been hit, but knew there was no slowing the man on this chase. Then he realized he had thought of his son as a man and knew it to be true. A slight shake of his head brought a faint grin to his face, as he realized his son was as much of a man as he himself was when he first came west. He nodded to himself as pride filled his heart.

Nothing was slowing Sean in his chase, but as they hit the end of the valley, the trail crested a slight rise and dropped into a wide timbered draw. When they broke through the thicker juniper, he was suddenly confronted by another warrior, standing beside his mount as he let an arrow fly. Sean dropped to the side and the arrow whispered past, but he drew his Colt and shot the warrior as he raced by. The warrior fell back against his horse, and in that quick glance, Sean saw the red blossom on the man's chest, but also the broken leg of the horse. But he dug heels into Dusty's ribs, asking for more. He knew they were closing on the captor and thought only of Fawn.

A quick glimpse through the trees and Sean leaned back against the cantle of his saddle as he pulled tight on the reins, bringing Dusty to a bouncing stop behind a large juniper. He looked to see Spotted Tail stopped in the open, facing back towards Sean, and holding Fawn before him, his arm around her waist. The horse stood, head down, sides heaving, staggering. Spotted Tail held his rifle, butt on his leg, muzzle up, and shouted, "White man! You want this woman? Come for her!" but his words were in Lakota and Sean didn't know the language, but he understood the intent.

Sean stepped down from Dusty, grabbing his Spencer as he did, and turned toward the taunting captor. Tate was behind him, "Careful son, he's got nothin' to lose and you do."

"I got to, Pa, but watch out for them other two, we don't know where they went."

Sean stepped around the juniper and stood, rifle at his hip. "You!" he pointed at Spotted Tail, "We let you go once, this time you'll die!"

Fawn translated Sean's words to Lakota and the man snarled. He looked past Sean to see Tate standing, rifle ready, and knew Sean's words were true. He knew he could not kill them both, and a quick glance at the trees and the rattle of hooves on stone told of another man coming. He snatched at the reins of his horse, tried to jerk his head around, but the horse fought back, stumbled to the side and fell to his knees, unseating both Fawn and Spotted Tail as they slid to the ground. The horse was between them and the white men, and Spotted Tail dropped his rifle across the horse's back for a quick shot at Sean.

When the horse stumbled, Sean stepped forward, bringing his rifle up as he leaned into his shot, and in that instant both rifles barked and spat smoke. Fawn had jerked free from the Sioux and dropped behind the downed horse. Sean's bullet took the Indian just in front of his ear, but plowed through the bear greased hair and took his scalp lock as it made a fist sized hole where it exited.

Fawn jumped to her feet and ran to Sean, almost knocking him over as she wrapped her arms around his neck and kissed him full on the mouth. His eyes wide, he leaned back and looked at the frantic woman that refused to let him pull away, and grinned as he hugged her tight. When he winced, she leaned back, saw the blood at his side, "You're hurt!"

"Ummhumm, a little, but I reckon I'll be alright. 'Course, you might have to tend to my wound a little." He grinned as she looked at him, trying to determine his intent. But when the corners of his mouth pulled back into a grin, she let an answering smile paint her face as she pulled him close for another hug, caring little about getting his blood on her tunic.

Tate and Jacques stood side by side, watching the two, "I think they kinda like each other, don'tchu?" asked Tate.

"*Mais Oui,* it would appear."

TWILIGHT LAY against the hillsides when the three horses

rounded the point of the finger ridge to approach the wagon camp. They were less than twenty yards from the wagons before the cry rose, "They're back!" Tate recognized the gravelly voice of Bucky and saw his big form step between the freight wagons. A pillar of smoke rose from the cookfire and the returnees dropped from their horses, tired and hungry. Sean threw a leg over the pommel and slid to the ground, turned to help Fawn to the ground, and caught her around the waist as her feet touched the grass. She leaned against him, arm around his waist, and looked down at his side.

THEY HAD TAKEN the time to clean and dress his wound, and Fawn rinsed the blood from his buckskin shirt in the stream at the valley floor. He stood tall and proud beside her as Red Leaf knelt beside the cookfire, looking stoically at the pair. Leaf looked to her man as he walked toward her, he shrugged his shoulders with his head cocked to the side and showing a grin, and she looked back to the couple, smiled and greeted her man with a hug.

As they seated themselves around the cookfire, Fawn helped her mother dish up some stew and coffee for the men. When each one had their plates and cups, Tate spoke, "How 'bout we say a word of thanks to the Lord for what He's done this day?"

"*Mais Oui!* declared Jacques as he removed his hat and bowed his head.

CHAPTER TWENTY-NINE
RETURN

THE MORNING OF THE THIRD DAY FROM THEIR BUFFALO CAMP, the four wagons drew up outside the walls of Fort Laramie. With no need to replenish supplies before making it to Fort Bernard, Tate wanted to report to the commandant about the attack by the Sioux. With no fanfare, he was ushered into General Harney's office to be greeted by the stern expression of the commandant.

"What's this that my aide says, you were attacked by some Sioux?!" he demanded.

"That's right," answered Tate as he took a chair at the General's direction.

"Details, man, details!"

Tate sat back, crossed one leg over his knee and began, "Well, it all started when a lone Ogalala shot one of the slaves at our noon stop. He was a young buck an' wantin' to steal some horses to pay a bride price."

"And you know all this how?" demanded the impatient officer.

"I caught up with him, brought him back to the wagons and questioned him."

"Where is he now?" growled Harney.

"We let him go."

"You what?!?!" shouted the man, standing to his feet and leaning over his desk toward Tate.

In a calm voice, he answered, "We let him go. Didn't have any need to keep him."

"So, your big Indian attack was one man!"

"No, that came later."

"Well?" insisted the exasperated commandant.

"We were hit by about fifteen warriors, maybe more. One of 'em was the same one that tried to take a couple captives the other side of Fort Bernard. Far as I could tell, they were all Brulé."

"And?"

"They hit us, we killed most of 'em, well, all 'cept two, and we lost one man."

"Who'd you lose? Anybody important?"

Tate knew what the General was thinking and that he was concerned for the young men he met when they came through before, but he also thought how easy it is for people like the general to think some lives are more important than others. He had seen that attitude before among the collegians and others that had risen to some position of prominence and thought themselves superior. He dropped his head and answered, "Louis Reale, the nephew of Thomas Scott, the one connected to the railroad." Tate watched as the General leaned back in his chair, obviously relieved the life lost was not one of the *more important* ones, like the Vice President's relation or one of the others.

Tate slowly shook his head and stood, "If that's all General, I'll be leaving. We want to make Fort Bernard 'fore dark."

The commandant stood, extending his hand from behind the desk, "Yes, yes. Well, we'll be on the lookout for any more of those Sioux attacks, but it sounds to me like you gave 'em a good licking! That's what they need, for certain. And was your buffalo hunt successful?"

Tate chuckled, "After the set-to with the Sioux, these city boys kinda lost their appetite for hunting and exploring the west. So, they'll be headin' back to what they call civilization."

The General grinned, knowingly, as the two shared a moment of understanding. But the difference between the two men was greater than the commandant thought. While the man in uniform sought a return to the east and civilization, the man in buckskins longed for the solitude of the mountains.

WHEN THE MEN of the wagons saw Tate come from the big gate of Fort Laramie, they climbed back into the wagons or on their horses and at the wave of his hand in the air, they were once again on the road. Sean and Fawn were in the lead, riding within arms-length of one another and always smiling. Jacques and Red Leaf followed but nearer the wagons than the scouting pair. Most of the college men had taken to being outriders to the sides of the wagons, and the slaves and others handled the teams.

Tate dropped back, making a check on each of the wagons as they passed, but when the first freighter drew near with Bucky at the lines, the big man hollered, "Tie off your horse and climb aboard. Wanna talk to ya!"

The road was well-traveled, and they passed another wagon train about mid-way between the two forts. With over twenty wagons and hopeful faces on all the pilgrims, Tate waved at most and wondered how many graves would decorate the plains and if any of the rest would make it all the way to Oregon before the winter snows trapped them in the mountains. He shook his head as he climbed aboard the big freighter to sit next to Bucky.

The big man grinned at Tate, slapped reins to the mules, and the creak and groan of the wagon, the rattle of trace chains, and the clomp of the mules' hooves on the hard-packed trail gave promise of their soon arrival at Fort Bernard. Tate leaned back against the wagon seat, propped his feet on the footboard and stretched his legs. "Been a long way, hasn't it, Bucky?"

"It has that, Tate. But I gotta admit, early on I had my doubts 'bout you an' the boy, there. My idea of an old mountain man is some grizzled ol'coot with whiskers coverin' his belly, tobacco juice in his beard, bow-legged, and meaner'n a mad wolverine!"

Tate chuckled, "I was followin' you till you got to the wolverine part. But I tangled with one o' them and I ain't never seen anything as mean!"

Bucky laughed, looked sideways at Tate, and started, "I been watchin' you an' the boy."

"Oh?"

"Yeah, ya see, my ol man was kinda like you, you know, spendin' time prayin' an' such, but then, unlike you, he spent most o' the day Bible thumpin' and beatin' on us kids. Got to where I couldn't take it anymore and me'n muh brother took off. I was twelve an' Freddy was ten, but we figgered we could make it on our own. But he caught up to us an' gave us a lickin' that liked to take muh hide plumb off. Freddy never did recover from that, an' after he died, me'n muh momma snuck off one night. Took the wagon, milk cow, and the shotgun. When muh ol' man caught up to us, he jerked Ma off'n the wagon an' started beatin' on her with his fists! He got me so angry, I figgered I had to stop him, and I grabbed up the shotgun and blew him to kingdom come! Ma pulled herself together, spit on his body, and climbed back on the wagon with nary a word. When we got to that little ol' town, we went to the livery, an' Ma bought me a horse an' saddle, handed me the shotgun and told me to git! Ain't seen or heard from her since."

Tate sat silently, waiting.

"Ain't never told nobody that afore." He slapped reins to the mules, hollered, "Move on, mules!" He turned to Tate, "Now you, you're different. I mean, I seen you prayin' and such, but what you have seems to be real. I don't understand it, but you strike me as a real man, I mean, honest and such. Like what you got with the Lord is what it's s'posed to be, am I right?"

"Yes, you're right. I mean as far as what you said about what I've got with the Lord an' all. That's called faith. I know God is real and that He answers prayer and guides us through this life."

"Alright, then. Here's what I wanna know. After what I done, killin' my pa and all, can God forgive me for that? Cuz, I know he needed killin' if anybody did, an' I had to do it, or he'da killed muh ma, but still . . . "

"Bucky, God can forgive anything."

The big man twisted around in his seat to face Tate, looking into his eyes for any doubt, and asked quietly, "Really?" as a tear started in one eye. He rubbed his eyes with his sleeve, looked back at Tate and asked, "Is there sumpin' I need to do, you know, like pray or sumpin'?"

Tate smiled and answered, "Bucky, what you did was sin, and sin has a price, and that price is death."

Bucky's head jerked around, but Tate continued, "But, God sent His son Jesus to pay that price for all of us when He died on the cross. It was for your sin and mine that Jesus died. And because He did, He also bought us a gift, the gift of eternal life. What that means Bucky, is if you really are wanting His forgiveness and want to know Heaven as your eternal home, then He tells us how. See, God knows your heart, and if you just ask, in prayer, for God to forgive you of all of your sins and ask for that gift of eternal life, then He will do just that. He'll forgive you, give you the gift , and more than that, He'll be your savior for all of eternity, starting today."

"Just like that? It's that easy?" asked the wondering seeker.

"It's that easy. That's so anyone and everyone can understand and do as He asks."

"Could you show me how? I mean, to do that, ask forgiveness an' such?"

"Of course. How 'bout I just lead us in prayer, an' you can say the same thing as I do, if you want, but it doesn't even have to be out loud, as long as you mean it."

"Alright, go 'head."

Tate began his prayer, and as he led Bucky in his words, the man asked God to forgive him and to give him the gift of eternal life, and the two men said "Amen" together. The big man looked over to Tate, grinning so wide Tate thought he would split his face, and he stuck out his meaty hand and shook Tate's enthusiastically.

"Thank you, thank you. That's a big load off. Thanks."

Tate stood to his feet and stepped down from the wagon box, dropping to the ground without the wagon slowing, waved to Bucky and slipped the tie of Shady's reins and mounted up.

Once aboard his horse, he stood in his stirrups and saw the tops of the buildings of Fort Bernard ahead, and gigged Shady to a canter to go to the head of the wagons to direct them to the warehouse for unloading.

"WAL, LOOK WHO'S BACK!" THE GREETING CAME FROM JOHN Richards, leaning lazily in the frame of the warehouse door. "I thought you all would be gone at least a month or more. Fill up already, didja?" He stepped from the doorway and walked toward Tate who was stepping down from his saddle.

"Not 'zackly. The boys got a little baptism by fire, an' it didn't quite suit 'em. Can't say's I blame 'em though."

Richards looked askance to Tate as they turned to walk shoulder to shoulder to Richards trading post complex. Once inside, John pointed Tate to a back room and the two friends were seated as John waved to a Mexican woman who had been his long-time housekeeper and cook. She went to the adjoining room and returned with steaming cups of coffee, handed them off and disappeared into the trade room.

"So, tell me all about it!" insisted John as he lifted the cup to his lips, looking at Tate.

Tate gave Richards a quick recap of the previous two weeks and finished with, "So, I get to turn these great adventurers over to you and you, my friend, can see to getting them back to Saint Louis!"

"Well, then, looks like we have two problems to resolve."

"Two?" asked Tate.

"Well, Louis Reale was the owner of those slaves, as far as any record shows, and where we sit is in unorganized territory where slavery is not allowed by proclamation. Leastways, not till either Kansas or Nebraska Territory claims this part of the country and then decides whether they're gonna be free or slave. So, we don't have any authority to send them boys back. Any ideas?" asked John.

"You know, I've thought about it a time or two, but didn't rightly know what to do. But, don't you make trips down to Sante Fe ever now an' then?"

"Ummhumm, and I've got a place down there that could use some more workers, inside and out, and they would be free down there. I see what'chur thinkin' Tate. Alright then, problem number two, getting these college boys home." He looked to his friend, waiting for an answer.

"Not so different. You take some wagons south to Sante Fe and drop those boys off in Colorado to catch the stage back east. Problem solved!"

Richards grinned, shaking his head at his friend. "You need to leave the mountains and come to work for me. I'd put you in charge of all the freighters and goin' to Sante Fe and St. Louis, and I'd stay here and grow fat and rich!"

"I wouldn't do that to a good friend. Why, you need to get out and about your own self, besides, this business would go bankrupt without you runnin' things."

Richards snapped his fingers and looked to Tate, "I almost forgot! You've got a letter!"

"A letter? Me?" both men were standing as Richards went to his desk and opened a drawer. He pulled out an envelope, handed it to Tate, "From Maggie!"

Tate grinned ear to ear, excited to hear from his redhead, looked up to Richards, "I'm gonna be at the camp over by the trees with Jacques and family. Come by later and we'll talk!" He didn't wait for an answer, but strode excitedly out of the trading post, walked to the warehouse and stepped back aboard Shady to go to the camp of Jacques and family, where he knew he would find Sean.

As he approached, he waved the envelope in the air as he looked at Sean, "Gotta letter from your ma!"

As he stepped down, Tate saw Red Leaf filling the plate of Jacques and Fawn was pouring coffee for them all. He walked close and said, "Something smells almighty good!"

"Don't it though?" answered a grinning Sean, "Fawn cooked it! It's got venison,

yampa, potatoes, onions, beans, cornmeal, and I don't know what all. But it sure is good!"

Tate sat down on a low stump, accepted a full plate, looked at the offering and smiled. It looked like a stuffed cornbread, with meat, and fixings, and his first mouthful confirmed Sean's proclamation. Tate grinned and nodded his head as he made short work of the plateful. After a second helping, both Sean and Tate were grinning and sat back, savoring the meal. As they started to hand their plates back to Fawn, she dropped a big spoonful of mixed berries on the plates for desert, which the men gladly devoured.

As he accepted another cup of coffee, Tate looked to Jacques, "Have you thought anymore about my proposition?"

"*Oui*, and both of the women were happy to hear. We will gladly join you!" declared Jacques.

Sean frowned as he looked from Jacques to his pa, and asked, "What?"

Tate grinned, "I thought you and I could use some company this winter, so I asked our friends here to come with us to the cabin for the winter."

Sean let a slow grin cross his face, then looked quickly to a smiling Fawn and back to his pa then forced a frown, "But

Pa, if we eat cookin' like this all winter, we'll be fatter'n hibernatin' bears!"

Everyone laughed and began chattering as they talked about the mountains, the cabin, and the coming winter. Tate drew back and pulled out the letter, straddled the crumbling cottonwood log and began reading.

My dearest Tate and Sean,

I hope this letter finds you both well and happy. Sadie and I are adjusting to city life, Sadie more than I, but adjusting, nevertheless. Sadie will start school soon, and I will be sharing the duties of running the Inn with your blessed Aunt. I do miss the mountains, but I want you to know I have been keeping up on my shooting practice. Just the other day I had an opportunity to try a moving target. It all began when ...

"GOOD MORNING, ladies. My name is Malcolm Whitehurst, and this is my companion, Erastus Throckmorton." Both men doffed their hats and nodded their head in deference.

"Gentlemen, are you in need of lodging or a meal?" asked LaVinia Finney, Maggie stood nearby.

"Oh, your Inn has been highly recommended for your fine dining. We are on our way, returning to St. Louis, and we are expected. So, if it is alright, we would certainly enjoy a meal at your fine table."

LaVinia turned to Maggie, "Would you show these gentlemen to a table please?"

"Certainly. This way gentlemen."

As they moved toward the table, Malcolm asked, "Did she say your name was Maggie?"

Maggie did not respond, but stopped by a table, placed the menus before the chairs, nodded and left without answering.

LaVinia had watched the men and as Maggie turned to

leave, she saw them looking at her and talking rather animatedly to one another. When Maggie came to her dais, LaVinia asked, "Did they say something to you?"

"Yes, the blonde one asked if you said my name was Maggie. I ignored him."

"Good. There's something about them I don't like. Although they look and act like perfect gentlemen, I don't like the way they looked at you!"

"Nor did I. Will you excuse me just a moment, there's something in my room I forgot."

"Surely."

When Maggie returned, she appeared calm and reserved, gave a quick glance toward the two men, then turned away from them to speak to Aunt Vinny. "As I thought, those are two of the men that Tate wrote about that had caused problems and left the group. I think they're up to no good."

"Well, then. Let's be very careful and take no chances with them. Since it's mid-afternoon, and there are no other guests yet, we don't know what they may try."

It was just a short while later when both men stood, placed their napkins at their plates, and turned to go to the front door. The dais stood back from the door and held the menus and other items for the Inn and also served as the station for the ladies as they directed the guests to the tables or to the rooms.

Malcolm strode boldly toward the women, Erastus holding back and showing himself nervous. Malcolm passed LaVinia and stood directly in front of Maggie, "You insulted me when you did not answer me! I asked if your name is Maggie, is it?" he demanded, his face reddening and his eyes glaring.

"Now just a minute young man! There's no need to be so rude!" declared LaVinia, stepping from behind the dais.

"You shut up! This is none of your affair!" growled

Malcolm, gritting his teeth as his nostrils flared and he curled his lip in anger.

Maggie looked at him, "Step away from me, now!"

"Malcolm, we should leave!" whined Erastus, standing near the door.

"Not until I show this, this . . . woman, what a real man is!" he snarled as he reached for Maggie's arm.

As the popinjay tried to grab her, from the fold of her dress Maggie brought up the pocket model Dragoon, unseen by the man, but he was suddenly stopped when he felt the barrel of the pistol thrust into his gut. He stopped and looked down, expecting to see her fist or open hand, but the sight of the gun barrel stopped him. He began to stutter and stammer, "Wait, wait, . . . " as he began to back step, looking for the door.

Erastus had fled when he saw the pistol and had already descended the stairs, grabbed the horse tethered at the rail, and was whipping it with the reins as he fled down the roadway.

Malcolm turned to flee and as he started to take the first step, Maggie shot the heel off his boot, and he fell face first down the steps. He scrambled to his feet, looking back wide eyed and terrified at Maggie and turned to flee. Once again, the Pocket Dragoon barked, and the other heel was cut from under the panicky man. His horse had spooked and jerked his rein free from the rail. The frightened man reached for the trailing reins, fell on his face again, scrambled to his feet and was last seen running and screaming, "wait, wait," down the long driveway frantically trying to catch the fleeing horse. .

So, you see, my dear husband. I have been keeping up with my target practice, and haven't missed one yet!

Tate was laughing loudly as he walked back to the fire. He finished reading the personal notes at the end of the letter, and looked up to an expectant group. He laughed again and shared the tale of the "real man" and his encounter with his redhead, much to the delight of everyone listening. John Richards had walked up to the group just as Tate started the story and he joined in the laughter of the others.

"You know, I never did like that curly-headed fop! And after he was gone, most of the others were relieved to be rid of him!" stated Richards.

Richards joined the group and they tucked the darkness away as they sipped the coffee and shared their tales.

"Massa Tate, we sure be thankin' you," stated Jeremiah, shaking Tate's hand enthusiastically and nodding to Horatio and Johnathan. "I neva thought I'd see the day when we was free!"

Tate grinned as he shook the old slave's hand, "Jeremiah, everybody should be free and maybe one day we'll both see the time when that's true. But, you'll have jobs waiting for you in Sante Fe and the three of you can start building yourselves a life. Who knows, maybe you can even have a family!" All three men laughed, and Horatio and Johnathan reached to shake Tate's hand as well.

Tate, Sean, and Jacques were saying their goodbyes to the men they traveled with and hunted beside. Men they would probably never see again, but men they had shared their lives and trials with, and hopefully men that had learned and grown because of those times. Patrick spoke for the others, "Tate, we'll never forget you and all we've done together. When we first met, I, and these others as well, were all very skeptical and judgmental. We doubted that a man in buckskins could teach us anything, but we were wrong. And we are very grateful to you," nodding his head toward Sean and Jacques to include them, "for everything. Thank you."

"Well, gentlemen, all we ask is that you do us proud. When we read about you in some out-of-date newspaper, I trust the news will be of good men doing great things."

Bucky had watched the three scouts saying their good-byes and he waited beside the big freight wagon for Tate's approach. He grinned as they neared, extending his meaty paw to shake his friends' hands in goodbye. As Tate grasped Bucky's hand, he asked, "Did Richards settle up with you on those hides?"

"He did. Although we had hoped to have a few more than we took, but that was our agreement. We split the total among the six of us, so at least we'll have a few coins to spend in Sante Fe."

"Well, here's a bit to add to the pot. We couldn't have done it all without you and we appreciate your help." He pressed two twenty-dollar gold pieces into the big man's hand and was pleased to see the wide-eyed surprise. "If you ever find yourself goin' over South Pass, you take the cut-off to the north and follow it to a big lake. You'll see a cabin to the west, and the coffee pot will always be on."

Bucky grinned and shook Tate's hand again. "I'll do that, by gum, I'll do that!"

Jacques, Tate, and Sean stood watching as the line of wagons and freighters pulled away from the fort. Bound to the south and eventually Sante Fe, the train would leave the collegians near Julesburg, Colorado, to catch the new east/west stage that traveled from Independence, Missouri to the goldfields of Colorado and back. But the former slaves would continue with the wagons to Sante Fe. Once there, they would be employed by John Richards at his warehouse and general store.

Tate turned to Sean, "Well son, looks like we can finally head home. I traded Richards for a couple of packhorses, and we've got enough to load 'em down, so, as soon as we get them ready, we're headin' for the mountains!"

"We can't get there soon enough, as far as I'm concerned," declared Sean as the three men turned back to the trading post of the fort.

"There are some things we must get also, but we should leave by mid-morning," responded Jacques.

THEIR CHOSEN route deviated from the Oregon Trail that followed the North Platte River to the north and west. Without the burdensome wagons, it was easier to head out due west and strike for the spine of mountains showing white tops on the horizon.

"By following the Laramie River, then the north fork of the Laramie, why, we'll save ourselves three, maybe four days travel time. Course, once we're across that long spine of mountains yonder, there's a pretty fair stretch of dry country. Ain't much green, but there is water, usually. But that way, we'll hit the Sweetwater, an' follow it to South Pass and then it's just a hop, skip, an' a jump, an' we'll be home!" explained Tate as they stretched out on the trail. Tate and Jacques were in the lead, followed closely by Red Leaf leading their one packhorse. Then Sean and Fawn rode together, each trailing a single packhorse.

"It'll take us 'bout a week, mebbe a little longer, dependin', to reach the Sweetwater. Then, oh, 'bout another week, maybe less, to get to the cabin," he explained. "You're gonna like it there, Jacques. From the front porch we can look out over the lake, watch moose an' elk come down to water, see the sun come up ever' mornin', yup, wonderful country."

"There is room for us to build a cabin also, no?" asked Jacques.

Tate turned in his saddle to look at his friend, "Uh, yeah, I reckon. Not that you'd need to, we got room."

"*Oui,* but it is good to have the privacy, yes?"

Tate grinned, understanding. "Yes, it is my friend. And there is plenty of room for as many cabins as you'd like to build. We'll help you an' we can get one up in no time. Lot'sa timber there, won't have to drag the logs far at all."

"Are there others there also?"

"There's a friend and his woman that have been stayin' there, mindin' things for me. I've got some mighty nice Appaloosa breeding stock there, and Whiskers and his woman, Red Pipe, have been stayin' in the cabin while we're gone."

"Will they stay?" asked the curious Métis.

"No, Whiskers likes to winter with his woman's people, the Arapaho. But they won't be too far."

THE FIRST PART of the week was the more difficult as they crossed the Laramie Mountains. The Laramie River, especially the north fork, carved a difficult path through the granite peaks leaving deep gorges and narrow canyons for the travelers to negotiate or circumvent. The crossing of the wide adobe basin that had an abundance of cacti, rattlesnakes, and big footed jackrabbits, was almost as challenging. With wide flat-topped mesas, rimrock, clay bottomed canyons, and endless dry flats, everyone was relieved to see the valley of the North Platte in the distance. "We'll cross the Platte yonder a ways," said Tate, pointing to the winding river in the flats, "and then we'll turn south and hit the Sweetwater. We should camp by it tonight!"

"Think we can get us some nice brookies for supper?" asked an excited Sean. The last week had been nothing but venison and most would welcome a change for dinner.

"Well, I guess that'll be up to you and whether or not you can fetch enough for all of us. But if you can, I for one would enjoy some tasty trout for supper."

They crossed the Platte just above a cascading waterfall and clambered over the rocky bank to reach the flats above the river. A wide stretch of boggy-bottomed marshland made them turn north to find a crossing of the meandering Horse Creek. They stopped for their nooning on the far side, giving the horses their first ample graze of deep green grass since they crossed the Laramie Mountains.

Leaf and Fawn mixed some cat-tail root with the pemmican, fashioning flat cakes to fry and gave the group a different, but tasty, noon meal. Fawn had busied herself picking strawberries, raspberries, and gooseberries, and everyone had a double handful of sweets for the day.

Tate sat on a flat rock beside the grassy bank. Tall grass waved in the breeze, but he watched the movement that went counter to the breeze, slow, moving along the edge of the grasses, stopping, and moving again. He knew what was moving in the grass and he waited and watched until a yellow and brown, fat bullsnake slithered toward the willows. He chuckled as he watched the almost eight-foot-long reptile search for its next meal. Tate knew the bullsnake wasn't venomous, but he shivered at the looks of the winding serpent as it made its getaway. He didn't like snakes of any kind, even the little garter snakes, harmless though they may be, were not his favorite creatures of the wild. And rattlesnakes, well, he saw no useful purpose for them.

He thought of Maggie and how she shared his distaste of

the scaly creatures. He knew he was going to miss Maggie and Sadie, maybe that was why he invited the Bottineau's to spend the winter. At least there would be someone to keep the lonesomeness at bay. He breathed deep, stood, and looked around. He walked to the top of a slight mound nearby, stood with one hand on his hip and the other shading his eyes as he scanned the flats that straddled the Sweetwater and beyond. Something caught his eye and he squinted and unconsciously leaned forward a little, trying to make out what he had seen. He turned around and trotted to where Shady was grazing. He had loosened the cinch on his saddle, let the reins trail, and gave Shady the opportunity to get his fill of the green grass.

Tate pulled the scope from his saddle bags, and returned to the slight rise. He focused on the spot that had caught his attention, leaned back to rest his elbow on his rib cage to stabilize his hold, and examined the thin wisps of smoke that climbed lazily toward the clouds. One pillar of white told of a cookfire, but there were several. Either a troop of cavalry or a band of Indians, but Indians wouldn't make that much fire for a midday meal, though soldiers would. But what would soldiers be doing out here? The nearest posts were Fort Bridger to the west and Fort Laramie in the east, both at least a week's ride away.

When Tate walked back to the cookfire, Jacques saw he was disturbed and asked, "What is it? What did you see?"

"Smoke, too much smoke. Unless there's a troop of soldiers there, I'm thinking there's a problem of some kind, maybe natives."

"We are no longer in Lakota lands are we?"

"No, this is Crow or Cheyenne, maybe Arapaho, country."

"Perhaps we should go see, no?"

Tate nodded his head, looked at the others, and started

for his horse. "I'll ride on ahead, but you come on along. If there's any trouble, I'll come back."

Sean had watched his father and knew his somber expression told more than his words. His pa was worried, and Sean wanted to go with him, but when he started to speak, Tate held up his hand, "No, I know you want to come with me, but it's best if you stay with the others. If there is a problem, they'll need your help." Sean lifted his chin, understanding what his pa didn't say, and with a slight nod, agreed to his responsibility.

To the southeast, the Sweetwater River wound its way toward its confluence with the Platte. On the northwest was a kidney shaped playa lake, surrounded by wide stretches of white alkali. Tate sat astride Shady, leaning forward on the pommel of his saddle, as he looked at the thin spirals of smoke twisting toward the blue canopy. It wasn't a group of cookfires of soldiers like he hoped to find, but the remains of a wagon train. Smoldering hulks of wagons, charred wood, twisted pieces of metal that held the dreams of pilgrims were all that remained. Other piles of black showed remnants of treasured possessions, a metal plowshare, broken pieces of mirror from a dresser, shattered pieces of dinnerware, and scattered strips of dress material. From where he sat, he could look to the south and see the hulk of Independence Rock, the halfway point of the Oregon Trail and he thought, *They didn't quite make it halfway.*

It was not an unfamiliar scene to Tate but still a disturbing one. The charred bodies of farmers and storekeepers were unrecognizable, even if there were any survivors to make that claim. But what disturbed him most was the frail figures of a little girl still clutching a ragdoll, and a little boy, barefooted, in high water britches, no shirt under his galluses, but holding tight to a carved toy rifle.

Tate slipped his neckerchief up over his nose and mouth, shook his head, and gigged Shady forward. Surely, he could find a shovel to start the burials. He didn't want to have to do it, but they must be buried before the carrion eaters turned a blind eye to the smoldering fires and began taking their liberties with the bodies. Most of the shovels were strapped to the sides and had burned with the wagons, but after scrounging around a while, Tate found two and selected a spot to start digging.

It was a gruesome task, but with everyone working, as dusk fell they stood by the mass grave and Tate recited the twenty-third psalm and everyone said "Amen," to finish the work. The afternoon had been spent with little conversation, but a lot of thinking and reminiscing, as is so often done at grave-sides. They knew this was the wagon train they passed near Fort Bernard just over a week ago. When they mounted to leave, Tate led them across the Sweetwater to follow the well-established trail of the Oregon bound wagons. They rode in silence, passed Devil's Gate, and camped near the Sweetwater. Leaf and Fawn let it be known that before any cooking was done, they were going to take a bath in the river. The men looked at one another, at their own clothes and blackened hands and Tate said, "That sounds like a good idea. But, we better wait and take turns. I don't want any of those," nodding his head back the way they came, "coming up on us while we're up to our chins in cold water!"

While they waited on the women, Jacques asked, "Do you know what tribe attacked the wagons?"

"I'm pretty sure it was Cheyenne. I found a couple arrows," said Tate, turning to retrieve a part of a shaft from behind the cantle of his saddle. He handed it to Jacques, "See the fletching, those are turkey feathers. The Cheyenne are known for that. Course, sometimes the Crow and Sioux use them, but it's only the bands out here in the flats that have turkeys. Up in the mountains, the Arapaho, Shoshoni, Black-feet, and others, use hawk, eagle, even duck feathers. And the markings, few though there are, makes me think Cheyenne. General Harney said the Sioux and the Cheyenne have been allied and are striking some of the settlers farther north. I am surprised they hit this far south, but, none of 'em are too happy with the reservation idea. I believe we'll see a lot more of that sorta thing before this is all over. There's just too many folks comin' out here and wantin' what they think is free land."

"*Oui*, I understand, but what can be done?"

Tate shook his head, "Nothin', I'm afraid."

They had stripped the gear from the horses, tethered them within reach of water and graze, and started a small fire for supper before the women, refreshed and smiling, came from the willows and the stream beyond. The men chose to bathe one at a time, leaving two on watch, while the women prepared the evening meal. Before long, the stars lit their lanterns, the moon peeked over the eastern horizon, and the cicadas chattered the travelers to sleep.

BY THE END of the week, the group of five rode into the clearing by the cabin and hailed the two sitting in the rockers on the porch. "Ho! Whiskers! Red Hawk!"

The big man stood, grinning and with his arm around his wife, raised one hand and hollered back, "Welcome home! It's been a long time!"

"Yes, it has, but we're home now," declared Tate as he pointed Shady to the corral behind the cabin. He motioned for the others to follow and as they passed the corner of the house, Tate introduced the others.

"And who is this man? You left with a boy and you return with a man!" said the big mountain man, looking at a grinning Sean.

"Ah, Whiskers! It's just me, Sean!"

"Oh, I see. And I see you have brought a woman also!"

Sean grinned and followed his pa to the corrals. They were happy to be home, but there was much to be done, but it would be pleasurable work, building and preparing for the winter. And the shared thought of a warm fire in a cozy cabin with a blanket of white outside brought a smile to the men. As Tate looked at his son he thought, *It may be a lonely winter, but the future holds promise.*

TERRITORY TYRANNY (ROCKY MOUNTAIN SAINT 11)

The next installment in the Rocky Mountain Saint, available March 2019 from B.N. Rundell and Wolfpack Publishing.

ABOUT THE AUTHOR

Born and raised in Colorado into a family of ranchers and cowboys, B.N. Rundell is the youngest of seven sons. Juggling bull riding, skiing, and high school, graduation was a launching pad for a hitch in the Army Paratroopers. After the army, he finished his college education in Springfield, MO, and together with his wife and growing family, entered the ministry as a Baptist preacher.

Together, B.N. and Dawn raised four girls that are now married and have made them proud grandparents. With many years as a successful pastor and educator, he retired from the ministry and followed in the footsteps of his entrepreneurial father and started a successful insurance agency, which is now in the hands of his trusted nephew. He has also been a successful audiobook narrator and has recorded many books for several award-winning authors. Now finally realizing his life-long dream, B.N. has turned his efforts to writing a variety of books, from children's picture books and young adult adventure books, to the historical fiction and western genres.